Meet Just William Again

Richmal Crompton, who wrote the original William stories, was born in Lancashire in 1890. The first story about William Brown appeared in *Home* magazine in 1919, and the first collection of William stories was published in book form three years later. In all, thirty-eight William books were published, the last one in 1970, after Richmal Crompton's death.

Martin Jarvis, who has adapted the stories in this book for younger readers, first discovered *Just William* when he was nine years old. He made his first adaptation of a William story for BBC radio in 1973 and since then his broadcast readings have become classics in their own right. BBC Worldwide has released nearly a hundred William stories on audio and for these international bestsellers Martin has received a Gold Disk and a British Talkies Award. An award-winning actor, Martin has also appeared in numerous stage plays, television series and films.

Meet Just William Again

Three books in one!

Adapted from
Richmal Crompton's original
stories by Martin Jarvis

Illustrated by Tony Ross

MACMILLAN CHILDREN'S BOOKS

William's Day Off and Other Stories first published 1999 by
Macmillan Children's Books
William's Haunted House and Other Stories first published 1999 by
Macmillan Children's Books
William the Great Actor and Other Stories first published 2001 by
Macmillan Children's Books

This edition published 2009 by Macmillan Children's Books
a division of Macmillan Publishers Limited
20 New Wharf Road, London N1 9RR
Basingstoke and Oxford
Associated companies throughout the world
www.panmacmillan.com

ISBN 978-0-330-46974-6

1 3 5 7 9 8 6 4 2

A CIP catalogue record for this book is available from
the British Library.

Typeset by SX composing DTP, Rayleigh, Essex
Printed and bound in the UK by CPI Mackays, Chatham ME5 8TD

Contents

Dear Reader

Ullo. I'm William Brown. Spect you've heard of me an' my dog Jumble cause we're jolly famous on account of all the adventures wot me an' my friends the Outlaws have.

Me an' the Outlaws try an' avoid our fam'lies cause they don' unnerstan' us. Specially my big brother Robert an' my rotten sister Ethel. She's awful. An' my parents are really _hartless_. Y'know, my father stops my pocket-money for no reason at all, an' my mother never lets me keep pet rats or _anythin'_.

It's jolly hard bein' an Outlaw an' havin' adventures when no one unnerstan's you, I can tell you.

You can read all about me, if you like, in this excitin' an' speshul new collexion of all my fav'rite stories. I hope you have a jolly gud time readin' 'em.

Yours truly

William Brown

William's Day Off

and Other Stories

Contents

William's Day Off

"They're slum children from London," said Ginger. "They've come for four days. They've never seen a cow, or anything like that."

"Well, there's not much to see in a cow," said William. "You can't have any fun with a cow. I've tried. Where did you say they were comin'?"

"To Eastbrook Farm. Mrs Camp's havin' 'em. They're sent by some sort of soci'ty what pays for slum children to come into the country, 'cause of the war."

"Well, I vote we take 'em round a bit, and show 'em woods an' cows an' things," said William.

"Miss Milton's sister's havin' 'em to tea

'safternoon," put in Henry. "I heard my mother say so this mornin'."

"Corks!" said William, aghast. "Fancy them havin' to waste an afternoon goin' to *her*."

Miss Milton had lent her cottage to her sister for the summer, and though William had not yet met the lady, he had received the discouraging news that she was almost an exact replica of her sister.

Next morning the Outlaws went over to Eastbrook Farm. They found two boys standing by the farm gate wearing grey shorts and grey jerseys. They looked very clean and very bored.

The newcomers it turned out were called Bert and Syd. They were ten and eleven years old.

No, they didn't think much of the country so far. A goat had butted them, and a gander had chased them. They were obviously disillusioned and homesick.

"You come along with us," suggested

William, "an' we'll show you some of our places."

"Don't mind if we do," agreed Bert cautiously.

Bert was the elder. He had a slight cast in one eye that lent him a slightly sardonic aspect, and a more than slight suggestion of adenoids.

Syd was small and gingery and obviously ready to follow Bert's lead unquestioningly.

"Don't mind if we do," Syd repeated.

They accompanied the Outlaws to the old barn, and any hostilities soon melted in the warmth of the Outlaws' friendliness. Two hours later, the six returned to the farm, firm friends.

"Tell you what we'll do this afternoon," said William. "We'll go over to Marleigh. There's some caves there an' we can play smugglers."

"Coo," said Bert regretfully, "I don't 'arf wish we could, but we can't. We've gotter go to tea somewhere this afternoon."

"A Miss Milton or somethin'," supplemented Syd.

"Huh, you'll have a jolly dull time there," William prophesied. "She's *awful*."

"She won't even give you a decent tea, if she's anythin' like her sister," said Ginger.

"She's worse then her sister," said Douglas gloomily. "I've seen her."

"Yes, but Mrs Camp'll make us go, I expect," said Bert.

All eyes turned to William.

"I say," he began, "s'pose two of us pretend to be Bert and Syd and go to tea at old Miss Milton's 'stead of them. It doesn't much matter for us, 'cause we can go to Marleigh Caves any day, but they've only got four days and it might rain on the others."

"She's seen me," said Ginger.

"And me," said Henry and Douglas.

"But she's *not* seen me," said William. "Tell you what. I'll say I'm Bert and that Syd's gotter cold or somethin', and then you can all go off to Marleigh Caves, and I'll go 'n' have tea with her, an' she'll never know it's not you."

"Coo," said Bert. "That's jolly decent of yer."

"Not 'arf," agreed Syd.

"Are you *sure* she's not seen you?" said Ginger.

"'Course I'm sure," said William. "And anyway, I'll make myself look different, same as actors and detectives do. Right then. We'll all meet at the ole barn, an' you an' me'll change clothes, Bert. And you can go to Marleigh Caves."

"Good egg!" cried Bert and Syd simultaneously.

William walked purposefully towards Miss Milton's house, intent upon the manipulation of his face.

He was representing Bert's slight cast by his best squint. Bert's suggestion of adenoids he represented by opening his mouth loosely to the size of a ping-pong ball.

In order further to disguise himself, he had damped his hair and brushed it into a straight fringe, and was walking with a curious, stooping, shambling gait, letting his hands dangle about his knees.

Miss Milton blenched slightly as she opened the front door.

"Please, ma'am," began William in a deep throaty voice. "Please, ma'am, I'm Bert, and Syd couldn't come. He's gotta bad cold."

He opened his eyes to their utmost

capacity, and fixed them on the end of his nose. He was finding his squint useful. It saved him from the necessity of meeting Miss Milton's eye.

"I'm sorry to hear that," said Miss Milton, conscientiously trying to overcome the distaste that his appearance inspired in her. Come in, dear boy. Wipe your feet well on the mat."

William followed her into the drawing room and sat down on a small chair by the window. Miss Milton looked at him, blinked, looked away, then, summoning all her courage, looked at him again.

"Are you enjoying your holiday in the country?" she said.

"Yes, ma'am," said William.

"I suppose you've never been in the country before, have you?"

"No, ma'am."

"It must be a delightful experience for you."

"Yes, ma'am."

"I hope you realise that you're a very lucky boy."

"Yes, ma'am."

Miss Milton tried to think of something else to say, but failed.

"Perhaps," she said at last, "you'd like to come out and see my sister's garden, would you?"

"Yes, ma'am," said William. He followed her out into the little garden.

"Now don't go on the grass," said Miss

Milton. "There's plenty of room for you to walk on the path."

William was tired of saying "Yes, ma'am". He was artist enough to want to make more of his part than that.

"Grass, ma'am?" he said, in his deep throaty voice. "What's grass?"

Miss Milton was taken aback. Surely even slum children knew what grass was? But evidently they didn't. So she hastened to explain.

"That's grass," she said, pointing to her sister's sparse little lawn. "It's – well, it's just grass."

William began to feel that a certain amount of enjoyment might, after all, be extracted from the situation. He pointed over the hedge to a cow in the next field.

"What's that?"

"Why, that's a cow."

"What's a cow?"

Miss Milton sighed. But of course, it was quite natural that a slum child should never have seen a cow.

"It's – er – it's just a cow, dear. A cow is – it's just a cow."

Miss Milton's cat sauntered out of the kitchen door, and eyed William sardonically.

"What's that?" he said.

"A cat, of course," said Miss Milton rather sharply. "Surely you've seen cats at home?"

William realised that he was rather over-doing his town-bred ignorance.

"It's bigger than town cats," he said hastily.

The cat, who had recognised William, winked at him, and went indoors again. William thought wistfully of Marleigh Caves and wished that he was there with the others.

"And now, dear, it's time we went in to tea."

William resisted the temptation to say, "What's tea?" and followed her into the dining room.

It was, as Ginger had prophesied, a rotten tea. William soon emptied the plates, but Miss Milton did not have them refilled.

She looked at him. "I suppose you've seen an oculist about your – erm – squint?"

"Er – yes," said William hastily, doing it again. "It comes on worse when I'm hungry."

"But you've just had your tea."

William made no comment on this.

"Well, just stay here a moment," said Miss Milton. "I'll try and get a little companion of your own age. You'd like that, wouldn't you?"

William grunted non-committally and she went into the hall. He followed her to the door to listen. She was telephoning to Mrs Lane.

Two minutes later, William saw his sworn enemy, Hubert Lane, entering the garden gate. Escape was impossible. He sat there intensifying his squint and opening his mouth to the size of a cricket ball.

Miss Milton went to the door and returned followed by Hubert. Hubert looked at William and recognition leapt into his eyes, then died away again.

The boy had looked like William Brown at first sight, but on further inspection he obviously wasn't. His clothes were different; his mouth was different; his eyes were different.

"This is Bert," Miss Milton introduced him. "And this, Bert, is Hubert. Now, Hubert, I want you to take Bert on a nice quiet walk down the road and show him the country. You'll go with Hubert, won't you, Bert?"

"Yes, ma'am," said William.

His voice was different too, thought Hubert.

"Come back in a quarter of an hour," Miss

Milton called after them as they set off down the road.

"I say, Bert," said Hubert, "you're awfully like a boy I know called William Brown. I mean, you are just at first. He's an awful boy. My mother won't let me play with him. I jolly well scored one off him today. I'm sellin' some piebald mice, shillin' each, and he wants one and I won't sell him one. And he's as mad as mad. I say, I've got a jolly good idea—"

They were passing William's house, and Hubert stopped.

"—Let's play a trick on him. You go in and go round to the back and smash the window in the tool-shed. I heard his father sayin' that the next time he broke that window, he wouldn't have any pocket money for a month. It's a jolly good trick, isn't it? Go on, go on. Do it quick and then come out. I'll wait for you here. Go on."

William crept round the back of the house, watched by the sniggering Hubert.

Then, out of sight, he entered the back door, slipped upstairs, changed into one of his ordinary suits, brushed his hair back, and came out of the front door with his usual sturdy tread, whistling, his hands in his pockets.

Hubert, still crouching behind the hedge, did not see William until he was almost upon him.

"Oh, hullo, Hubert," said William. "What are you doing here?"

Hubert blinked, gasped, and looked wildly at the path down which he'd seen Bert disappear.

"Er – um – I say, William, there's a – er – a boy in your back garden. I was just taking him for a walk and he ran away from me down into your back garden. I – I – told him not to. I hope he's not doin' any damage."

"Oh, I'll go and have a look for him," offered William cheerfully, and set off down the path.

He returned almost immediately.

14

"There's no one there. Who did you say it was?"

"He must be there. He's a country holiday boy called Bert. He'd gone to tea at Miss Milton's, and I was just taking him on a nice quiet walk down the road when he suddenly ran in at your gate. I don't know why. I called out, 'Come back', but he went on. I say, do you mind if I come round an' look for him."

"No, come on and have a look."

Hubert peered nervously into the tool-shed and the summer-house, followed by the grinning William.

"He – he can't have gone anywhere else, can he?" said Hubert distractedly. "I don't know what I'm goin' to do if I don't find him."

"He might've fallen into the rain tub an' got drowned," said William helpfully.

Hubert's face turned pale green. "What am I going to do? I can't go back to Miss Milton's without him. And I can't just go home because she'll ring up my mother and there'll be an awful fuss. I say, William, you will help me, won't you? I've got an idea. This boy was a bit like you. Jus' a bit. If you can sort of cross your eyes and hang your mouth open a bit, an' walk sort of doubled up, she might think it was him. I bet Miss Milton's jolly short-sighted. People like her always are."

"But what about clothes?" said William.

Hubert's face fell, then lit up again.

"You could put on your raincoat, and I could say that it looked like rain so we called at the farm for your raincoat, and she won't notice you've not got the same things under-neath."

William considered, and then a light beamed suddenly in his eye, too.

"All right, I will, if you'll sell me one of your piebald mice."

Hubert hesitated. He had widely advertised his refusal to sell the mouse to William, and he would lose considerable face if he did so, but the crisis was an urgent one.

"Very well," he said.

"Here's the shillin'," said William. "You can go and fetch it now, and then I'll go with you to ole Miss Milton."

A few minutes later, William was hiding his piebald mouse carefully in a wooden box, with holes bored in for ventilation.

"Now, what d'you say this boy looked like?" he said in a businesslike tone, as he came out doing up the buttons of his raincoat.

"Well, he had a sort of squint, same as I told you."

William did a mild and tentative squint.

"What else?"

"His mouth sort of kept open all the time."

William opened his mouth to about the size of a ha'penny marble.

"Well, yes. I mean, it's jolly good. It's not *quite* like him, of course, but I bet she won't notice."

"Well, what do you want me to do? I've not got much time."

"Jus' come back to her with me and say you've had a jolly nice walk with me an' that sort of thing. An' that it's time you went home now. An' then go off down the road, as if you were going to Eastbrook Farm. An' then, if they say that this Bert never got home, she can't say it's my fault."

They walked down the road. Hubert's face grew paler as they approached Miss Milton's. The front door was open and Miss Milton was telephoning in the hall. She was evidently describing her guest to an acquaintance.

18

"Oh, he's just come in now," she said. "Hmm – he looks better already. Yes, come straight round. You have a little boy of your own, haven't you? Could he come too? Oh, he's out. Well, yes, I quite understand. But *you'll* come, won't you? You must of course be prepared for something very different from your own child."

She turned from the telephone to greet them.

"Well, dears."

William, with his modified squint, said that it was time he went home. Miss Milton, however, insisted on hearing a detailed account of their walk before he went.

"I suppose it opened a new world to you, didn't it, my boy?" she said to William.

Suddenly she looked out of the window.

"Oh, here's a lady who's kindly coming to see you, Bert," she said. "I'll just go and open the door."

They heard greetings in the hall, then the door was thrown open and, "This is Bert," said Miss Milton, pointing to him in a proprietary fashion.

William squinted wildly and opened his mouth almost to the size of a football, but in vain.

"*William!*" said Mrs Brown.

"'S not William," protested Hubert vehemently. "Honest. 'S not William. He's like William, but he's not William. It's Bert."

"Of course it's William," said Mrs Brown indignantly.

Hubert persisted that it was not William, and Miss Milton supported him. Mrs Brown said that a woman knew her own son after eleven years. William continued to squint and said nothing.

Then the real Bert, hot and breathless and dirty and gloriously happy, arrived. He'd had a wonderful afternoon at Marleigh, but on the way home had run into Mrs Camp who, discovering that he was wearing another boy's suit, had sent him to retrieve his jersey.

The altercation waxed fast and furious. Mrs Brown said that she knew nothing about Bert; all she knew was that William was William. Everyone talked at once, except William.

William waited patiently for the hubbub to subside. He'd have to give an account of himself soon enough. No need to precipitate matters.

Meantime, he was fixing his thoughts on the one bright spot in the whole situation. And the one bright spot in the whole situation was – the piebald mouse. Bert, or no Bert, that, at any rate, was safely his.

William's Goodbye Present

"Uncle Paul's goin' back to Australia tomorrow," said Hubert Lane. "I'm goin' to see him off at Hadley Station. He says he'll call round an' say goodbye to you on the way."

"All right," said William amicably.

There had been a lull in the hostilities between the Hubert Laneites and the Outlaws during the visit of Hubert's Uncle Paul from Australia.

For Uncle Paul was an uncle after the Outlaws' own heart, and he evidently much preferred the Outlaws to his own nephew and his nephew's friends.

To William, the visit opened up whole new worlds of adventure, and he had proved an apt pupil at whistle and boat making.

In fact, Uncle Paul had said that the last boat William had made was almost as good as he could have made himself.

"Now, what you want," he said, "is a good knife. I'll give you one before I go. I'll get you one like mine if I can."

"Like yours!" gasped William incredulously.

"Yes," said Uncle Paul, glancing carelessly at the magnificent weapon with which he had just fashioned a perfectly formed and perfectly balanced boat. "Those little penknives of yours are no good."

The next day he had said, "I've not forgotten that claspknife of yours. I went into Hadley about it, and they hadn't one in stock, but they're going to get one."

On the last morning of Uncle Paul's visit William was hanging about his front gate when the car containing Uncle Paul and

Hubert came down the road on its way to Hadley station.

Uncle Paul stopped the car and jumped out.

"I was coming to see you to say goodbye," he said to William. "We've had a great time together, haven't we? Don't forget what I told you about lighting fires. And when you're tracking down wild animals be sure you're the right way of the wind or they'll get your scent. Oh, and about your knife—"

"Yes?" said William eagerly.

"They said they'd have it in first thing this morning, so I'll stop the car at the shop in Hadley and get it, and Hubert here can bring it back to you. That'll be all right, won't it?"

"Yes," agreed William heartily, "an' I'm jolly grateful to you. I've wanted a knife like that all my life."

"Splendid!" said Uncle Paul. "I'm giving Hubert a pistol for his present – Well, goodbye. See you again next time I'm over."

He drove off, Hubert sitting beside him with a faint secret smile on his face.

William's sorrow at the departure of Uncle Paul was mingled with joy at the prospect of the possession of the magnificent claspknife.

But the morning passed by and Hubert did not appear with the claspknife. After lunch, William could restrain his impatience no longer and set out for the Lanes' house.

Mrs Lane greeted him without enthusiasm. She was tired of seeing him about the place. Paul had encouraged him too much.

"Well?" she said coldly. "What do you want?"

"I've come for my knife," said William simply.

"Your *what*?" she said.

"My knife," said William. "The knife that Hubert's Uncle Paul's given Hubert for me."

"I don't know what you're talking about," said Mrs Lane. "Hubert had a knife that his Uncle Paul gave him for a parting present, but I know nothing about any knife of yours. Hubert!" she called.

Hubert came slowly into the hall. His fat, pale face still wore the faint smile.

"I've come for my knife," said William sternly.

The smile spread all over Hubert's fat, pale face. "What knife?" he said.

"The knife Uncle Paul said he was giving you for me."

Hubert took from his pocket an exact, but shiningly new, replica of Uncle Paul's claspknife.

"Yes, that's it," said William eagerly.

But Hubert did not at once hand it over with apologies for the delay.

Instead, he slipped it back into his pocket with a careless air of proprietorship.

"That's my knife," he said. "He gave it me for a goodbye present."

"He said he was giving you a pistol for a goodbye present," said William indignantly.

Hubert took out a shining new pistol from another pocket.

"Yes," he smiled. "He gave me that, too."

William gazed at him blankly.

"But he *promised* the knife to me. You were there when he did. He said he'd call at the shop for it and give it you to give to me."

"He never did," said Hubert. "He never said anything about a knife when he called to say goodbye to you. He gave this knife to me. That's all I know."

William was, for a moment, struck speechless with horror. He turned indignantly to Mrs Lane.

"It *is* my knife," he said. "Uncle Paul told me he was going to give it to me. He was goin' to call for it in Hadley this mornin', and give it to Hubert to give to me. He told me so. Hubert was there when he told me so."

Mrs Lane looked at Hubert.

"Did he, Hubert?"

Hubert met her eye blandly.

"'Course he didn't," he said. "He's jus' makin' it all up to get the claspknife off me."

William stared at him.

"You *naughty* boy!" Mrs Lane was saying. "How *dare* you come here with a string of lies like this?"

"But he did," said William desperately.

"Be quiet. Go away at once, William Brown."

William knew that further protestation would be useless.

Stunned and bewildered, he walked gloomily to the old barn where he had arranged to meet the Outlaws, to show them his precious new possession. As soon as they saw him they knew that something was wrong.

Not thus – slowly, dejectedly, thoughtfully – does the owner of a brand new claspknife walk.

"Haven't you got it?" called Ginger as he approached.

"No," said William.

"Never mind," said Ginger. "I bet it'll have come before tonight."

"Oh, it's come," said William bitterly. "It's come all right."

They stared at him in astonishment. Why wasn't he swaggering, then? Why wasn't he displaying it?

"Where is it, then?" demanded Douglas.

"*He's* got it," said William.

"Who?"

"Hubert Lane," said William, spitting the name out as if it were some noxious draught.

They crowded round him in consternation as he told them the whole story.

Hubert, of course, had no real use for the claspknife. He was definitely not a claspknife boy.

He had taken so much trouble to obtain it only because William wanted it and he wanted to "score off" William. The pleasure he got out of it was in hanging out of his bedroom window, safe from attack, and displaying it to William and the Outlaws with jeering triumph whenever they passed down the road in front of his house.

It was just when William had almost given up hope of either getting back his knife or avenging the insult that an idea occurred to him. He remembered quite suddenly the weak spot in Hubert's armour. Hubert still believed in fairies and witches and spells.

There had been an historic occasion when he had even managed to persuade Hubert that he had been made invisible. Surely that weakness could be turned to account now?

He called a meeting of the Outlaws in the old barn, and together they formed a Plan.

The next morning William and Ginger stood in the road, in front of the Lanes' house.

William, assuming a nauseatingly pleasant expression, called up to Hubert's window, "Will you come out an' play with us, Hubert?"

Hubert appeared at his bedroom window. Ginger imitated William's nauseous expression.

"Come and play with us, Hubert," pleaded

Ginger. "It's all right. We've got a secret. We've not told anyone else yet. We'll tell you if you'll come."

Next to greed, Hubert's consuming passion was curiosity. They knew that he would now have no peace of mind till he had learnt the secret.

"All right," he said condescendingly. "I'll come along."

He vanished from the window and soon appeared at the gate.

"It's all right about that knife, Hubert," said William. "You can keep it."

"Thought you'd feel that way," said Hubert with an unpleasant sneer. He took out the knife from one pocket, the pistol from another, flourished them carelessly then restored them to his pockets.

The two Outlaws restrained themselves. They walked together until they reached the field by the old barn. William and Ginger led Hubert across the stile into the field.

"Well," said Hubert, "what's this secret of yours?"

"It's this," said William, lowering his voice. "When we came here this morning, we saw an ole woman in the field, with a cloak an' a big pointed hat an' a broomstick."

The superior sneer fell from Hubert's face.

"It was a witch," he said. "It was a witch, of course. What was she doin'?"

"She was jus' goin' about an' wavin' her broomstick an' sayin' things."

"Spells!" said Hubert, his round, credulous face pink with eagerness. "She was makin' spells. I say" – his eyes glinted greedily – "did she say anythin' about findin' treasure or anythin' like that?"

Walking by his side, William carefully led Hubert on to a spot that had recently been burnt brown by one of the Outlaws' camp-fires.

"She said somethin' over that bit you're walkin' on now," he said reflectively.

"What was it?" said Hubert.

"Well, it went somethin' like this," said William:

"Whoever treads upon this bit of burned,
Into a hen-coop shall his home be turned.

"And then it went on, somethin' about all the family that was in the house should be turned into hens an' anyone of the family who wasn't in it when the spell came on should be turned into hens the minute they saw the hen-coop."

Hubert's mouth dropped open and he leapt quickly away from the patch of burnt grass.

"W-w-w-what? A hen-coop?"

"Yes," said William, "but I don't suppose there's really anythin' in it. Go'n look if your house is turned into a hen-coop. You can see it from the stile, can't you?"

Hubert started forward, then remembered the second part of the spell, and returned.

"I'd better not," he said anxiously. "You go 'n' look," he added, turning to Ginger.

Ginger went down to the stile, from which he could see the solid four-square structure of stone and brick that was the Lanes' house.

"Crumbs!" he shouted in well-simulated horror. "It's gone. There's only a hen-coop."

Hubert paled.

"I don't b'lieve you; I d-d-d-don't believe you."

"Well, come and look for yourself," challenged Ginger.

Again Hubert remembered the latter part of the spell, and shook his head.

"No, I won't," he said. "You want to get me turned into a hen, that's what you want. Anyway, I don't believe you."

"Well, come and look for yourself if you don't believe me."

Matters having thus reached a deadlock, Douglas appeared, sauntering idly from behind the old barn.

"I say, Hubert," said Douglas airily, "what's happened to your house?"

"W-w-w-what?"

"It's gone," said Douglas. "I've just passed it now, an' it's gone, an' there's a hen-coop where it was, with a brown an' white hen scratchin' about outside it."

That was a clever touch of verisimilitude on Douglas's part. He had seen Mrs Lane through the window and she had been wearing a brown and white dress.

"Corks! That'll be Mother," said Hubert.

"I say, there's a hen jus' setting off from the coop an' going down the road," called Ginger from the stile.

"That'll be Father," moaned Hubert. "He goes to the station about this time."

"I bet they won't let him on the train," said Ginger. "Not like that."

Henry appeared suddenly in the road and vaulted the stile.

"I say!" he said. "Hubert's house has gone. "There's jus' a hen-coop there."

At this proof from yet another independent source, Hubert burst into tears. They crowded round, comforting him.

"Don't worry, Hubert. They have quite a good time, hens."

"You'll get to like worms an' grubs after a bit, I expect."

"You'd better go back an' get turned into one now an' get it over. You'll get used to it."

"I expect you're hungry aren't you, Hubert? You'd better go home an' have some nice grubs an' worms.

"I bet you'll get a bit tired at first, havin' to sleep on one leg, but it won't seem so bad after a year or two."

"I believe he's turning into one now, don't you? His face is gettin' jus' like a hen's."

Hubert's sobs turned into long howls.

"I d-d-don't want to be a h-h-h-hen, I d-d-d-don't want to be a h-h-h-hen."

"Well, listen, Hubert," said William kindly. "I heard this witch say somethin' else, after she'd said about the hens."

"W-what did she say?"

"Well," said William, "she went over to the stream here – an' she waved her broomstick over it an' she said:

"An' never shall he be free of the spell
Till he throws into here somethin' that cuts
an' somethin' that shoots as well."

Hubert blinked and considered. Then he plunged his hand into his pocket and brought out the claspknife.

"D'you think that'd do?" he said anxiously.

William examined it with a judicial air.

"It might," he said. "It cuts, anyway. No harm in tryin'. But what about the other? She said, 'Somethin' that shoots as well'."

From another pocket Hubert brought out his pistol.

"What about this? Would this do?"

"You might try," said William doubtfully. "Try throwin' 'em both in together—"

Pistol and penknife fell with a splash into the little stream. At once Ginger raised a cry from the stile.

"I say! Hubert's house has come back. That hen-coop's gone, an' Hubert's house has come back."

Hubert's fat, tear-stained face shone with relief.

"Corks!" he said. "I'm jolly glad you heard her say that end bit."

"She said somethin' else," said William. "She said that if ever you came here to look for 'em in the stream or if ever you told anyone about this hen business, you'd be turned into somethin' a jolly sight worse than a hen."

Hubert paled again.

"I won't," he said earnestly. "I jolly well won't – I promise I won't – I say! I don't look as if I'm turnin' into a hen now, do I?"

"No," William reassured him. "You're gone quite back to a boy again now."

Cautiously, fearfully, Hubert approached the stile. Then he gave a whoop of joy. "It *has* come back! It's all right. It has come back."

"Well, don't you forget about not tellin' anyone," William warned him.

"No, I won't," said Hubert fervently, "and I'm jolly grateful to you for remembering the end part, the part that turned it back. Worms!

I was jolly well dreadin' having to eat worms. Well, I'm goin' home, then, I'm jolly hungry. Worms!" he said again. "Ugh!" And he set off at his fat, slow trot, down the road towards the house.

The next morning, the Outlaws passed Hubert as he was standing at the gate. William held the claspknife and Ginger the pistol. Neither had been damaged by its brief immersion in the stream.

Hubert looked at them with interest. "Where did you get those?" he said.

William turned a bland, expressionless face to him. "The fairies gave them us," he said.

William Plays
Santa Claus

William walked slowly and thoughtfully down the village street. It was the week after Christmas. Suddenly he saw someone coming towards him.

It was Mr Solomon, the superintendent of the Sunday school of which William was a reluctant member.

William had just heard that Mr Solomon was going to form a band from the elder boys of the Sunday school.

William confronted him.

"Afternoon, Mr Solomon," he said.

Mr Solomon looked him up and down with distaste.

"Good afternoon, my boy," he said icily. "I am on my way to pay a visit to your parents."

This news was not encouraging.

William turned to accompany him and boldly broached the subject of the band.

"Hear you're gettin' up a band, Mr Solomon," he said casually.

"I am," said Mr Solomon, more icily than ever.

"I'd like to be a trumpeter," said William, still casually.

"You have not been asked to join the band," went on Mr Solomon, "and you will *not* be asked to join the band."

"Oh," said William politely.

They walked on.

"I am going," continued Mr Solomon, "to complain to your parents of your shameful behaviour on Christmas Eve, when you were supposed to be carol-singing."

"Oh – that," said William as though he remembered the incident with difficulty. "I remember – we . . . sort of lost you, didn't we?"

He and the Outlaws had, in fact, spent the evening in glorious lawlessness.

Mr Solomon turned in at the gate of William's home, and William accompanied him with an air of courage that was derived solely from the knowledge that both his parents were out.

He went round to the side of the house. His companion went up the front steps, rang the bell, and was invited in to tea by Ethel, William's grown-up sister.

William had forgotten that Ethel was at home, nursing a cold.

Ethel happened to be in the temporary and, for her, very rare position of being without a male admirer on the spot. Everyone seemed to have gone away for Christmas.

Mr Solomon was not, of course, a victim worthy of Ethel's bow and spear, but he was better than no one. Therefore she gave him tea and smiled upon him.

He sat, blushing deeply and gazing in rapt adoration at her blue eyes and Titian red hair.

He had not even dared to tell her the *real* object of his visit lest it should prejudice her against him.

William went indoors, assumed his most guileless expression, and entered the drawing-room. He sat down upon a chair next to Mr Solomon.

After a silence Ethel spoke without enthusiasm.

"Mr Solomon has very kindly come to make sure that you're none the worse after your little outing on Christmas Eve."

William turned his gaze upon Mr Solomon. Mr Solomon went pink and nearly choked over his tea.

Demoralised by Ethel's beauty and sweetness of manner he had indeed substituted for his intended complaint a kindly enquiry as to William's health.

William made no comment.

"That's very kind of him, isn't it, William?" said Ethel rather sharply. "You ought to thank him."

"Thank you," he said in a tone in which Mr Solomon perceived quite plainly mockery and scorn.

Another silence fell. Suddenly the clock struck five and Mr Solomon started up.

"Good heavens!" he said. "I must go. I ought to have been there by five."

"Where?" said Ethel.

"At the school. It's the old folks' Christmas party. I was to give out the presents – the mixed infants' party too – I'm afraid I shall be terribly late."

He looked about frantically.

"Oh, but can't someone else do it for you?" said Ethel. "It seems such a shame for you to have to run off as soon as you've come."

Mr Solomon looked into Ethel's blue, blue eyes and was lost.

He didn't care who gave away the presents to the old folks and the mixed infants. He didn't care whether anyone gave them away. All he wanted to do was to sit in this room and be smiled upon by Ethel.

It came to him suddenly that he'd met his soulmate at last.

"Isn't there anyone who'd do it for you?" said Ethel again, sweetly.

He thought for a minute.

"Well, I'm sure the curate wouldn't mind doing it," he said at last. "I've often taken his boys' club for him."

"Well, William could take the message to him, couldn't he?" said Ethel.

Glorious idea! It would kill two birds with

one stone. It would prolong this wonderful tête-à-tête and get rid of this objectionable boy.

Mr Solomon smiled upon William almost benignly.

"You'll do that, won't you, William?"

"Yes," said William obligingly, "cert'nly."

"Listen very carefully to me then, dear boy," said Mr Solomon. "Go to Mr Greene's house and ask him if he'd be kind enough to take over my duties for this afternoon as I'm – er – unable to attend to them myself. Tell him that the two sacks containing the gifts for the old folks' party and the mixed infants' party are in my rooms. The larger of the two is the old folks' party presents. He'll find in my rooms, too, a Father Christmas costume which he should wear for giving the old folks' presents, and a Pied Piper costume for giving the mixed infants' presents . . ."

William walked slowly down the road to Mr Solomon's rooms.

He had decided after all *not* to call upon

the curate. He had decided very kindly to perform Mr Solomon's two little duties himself.

He was most anxious to be admitted to Mr Solomon's band as a trumpeter, and he thought that if Mr Solomon found his two little duties correctly performed by William his heart might be melted and he might admit William as a trumpeter to his band.

Moreover, there is no denying that the thought of dressing up as Father Christmas and the Pied Piper and distributing gifts to old folks and mixed infants appealed very strongly indeed to William's highly developed dramatic instinct.

Mr Solomon's housekeeper admitted him without question and a few minutes later William staggered across to the school with two large sacks and two large bundles over his shoulders.

He found a small classroom to change in. It was intensely thrilling to put on the Father Christmas beard and wig and the trailing

red cloak edged with cotton wool.

He then carefully considered the two sacks. Why should the old folks have a larger sack than the mixed infants? he thought.

He shouldered the *smaller* sack therefore and set off to the old folks' party.

As he entered, old folks in various stages of old age sat round the room, talking to each other complainingly.

They were engaged in discussing among themselves the inadequacy of the tea, the

uncomfortableness of the chairs, the piercing-
ness of the draught, and the general dullness
of the party.

"'Tisn't what it used to be in my young
days," one old man was saying loudly to his
neighbours.

At the sight of William with his sack they
brightened.

A perspiring young man and woman
hurried down to him eagerly.

"So glad to see you," they gasped. "You're
awfully late – I suppose Mr Solomon sent you
with the things?"

Not much of William's face could be seen
through the beard and wig, but what could be
seen signified assent.

"Well, do begin to give them out," said the
young man. "It's simply ghastly! They won't
do anything but sit round and grumble. I hope
you've got plenty of tea and 'baccy. That's
what they like best."

William began, and it was not until he had
presented an outraged old man with a toy

engine that it occurred to him that it had been perhaps a mistake to exchange the two sacks.

But having begun, he went doggedly on with his task.

He presented to the old men and women around him dolls and tin motor cars and little wooden boats and garish little picture books and pencil cases – all presents laboriously chosen by Mr Solomon for the mixed infants.

The old folks were amazed and indignant. But there was something of satisfaction in their indignation. Something fresh to grumble at was almost in the nature of a godsend.

William gathered from the homicidal expressions with which the helpers were watching him that it would be as well to retire as hastily as possible.

He handed his last present, a child's paintbox, to an old woman by the door and departed almost precipitately.

Then the storm broke out and a torrent of shrill indignation pursued his retreating form.

He changed into the Pied Piper costume, retaining his Father Christmas beard and wig in order to better conceal his identity.

Then he shouldered his other sack and a few moments later he flung open the door of a room in which a few dozen mixed infants gambolled half-heartedly at the bidding of their conscientious helpers.

A little cluster of mothers sat at the end of the room and watched them proudly.

The mixed infants, seeing him enter with his sack, brightened and broke into a thin shrill cheer. A helper came down to greet him.

"How good of you to come," she said gushingly. "The procession first, of course – the children know just what to do – we've been rehearsing it."

The mixed infants were already getting into line. The helper motioned William to the head of it.

"Twice round the room, you know," said the helper, "and then distribute the presents."

William began very slowly to walk round the room, his sack on his shoulder, his train of mixed infants prancing joyously behind.

William's brain was working quickly. He had a strong suspicion that he would soon be distributing packets of tea and tobacco to a gathering of outraged mixed infants.

His hopes of being admitted into Mr Solomon's band faded.

Then, suddenly, he decided not to await meekly the blows of fate. Instead he'd play a bold game.

The mothers and helpers were surprised

when suddenly William, followed by his faithful band, walked out of the door and disappeared from view.

But an intelligent helper smiled brightly and said, "How thoughtful! He's just going to take them once round the school outside. I expect quite a lot of people are hanging about hoping for a glimpse of them."

"Who is he?" said a mother. "I thought Mr Solomon was to have come."

"Oh, it's probably one of Mr Solomon's elder Sunday school boys. He told me once that he believed in training them up in habits of social service. He's a wonderful man. I'm sure he'd have come if some more pressing duty hadn't detained him. The dear man's probably reading to some poor invalid at this moment."

At that moment (as a matter of fact) the dear man had got to the point where he was earnestly informing Ethel that no one had ever, ever, ever understood him in all his life as she did.

It wasn't until several minutes later that frenzied mothers and helpers poured out into the playground. It was empty.

They poured out into the street. It was empty. Everything was empty.

The old legend had come true. A Pied Piper followed by every mixed infant had vanished completely from the face of the earth.

Ethel had just sneezed, and Mr Solomon was just thinking how much more musically she sneezed than anyone else he had ever met, when the mothers and helpers burst in upon them.

They took in the situation at a glance and never again did Mr Solomon recapture the pedestal from which that glance deposed him.

But the immediate question was the mixed infants.

"B-b-but Mr Greene came to give the presents," gasped Mr Solomon. "It was Mr Greene."

"It certainly wasn't Mr Greene," said a helper tartly, "it was a boy. We thought it must have been one of your Sunday school boys. We couldn't see his face plainly because of his beard."

A feeling of horror stole over Mr Solomon. With a crowd of distracted mothers at his heels he returned to the school and conducted a thorough and systematic search. No mixed infants. The attitude of the mothers was growing hostile. They evidently looked upon Mr Solomon as solely responsible for the calamity.

"Sittin' there," muttered a mother fiercely, "sittin' there dallyin' with red-haired females while our children was bein' stole – *Nero!*"

"*'Erod!*" said another, not to be outdone in general culture.

"*Crippen!*" said another showing herself more up-to-date.

The perspiration was pouring from Mr Solomon's brow. It was like a nightmare.

"I – I'll go and look round the village," he said desperately. "I'll go to the police – I promise I'll find them."

"You'd better," said someone darkly.

He tore in panic down the road. He tore in panic up the nearest street. And then, suddenly, he saw William's face looking at him over a garden gate.

"Hello," said William.

"Do you know anything about those children?" panted Mr Solomon.

"Yes," said William calmly. "If you'll promise to let me be a trumpeter in your band, you can have them. Will you?"

"Y–yes," spluttered Mr Solomon.

"On your honour?" persisted William.

"Yes," said Mr Solomon. "Yes—"

"An' Ginger an' Henry an' Douglas – all trumpeters?"

"Yes," said Mr Solomon desperately.

It was at that moment that Mr Solomon decided that not even Ethel's charm would compensate for having William for a brother-in-law.

"All right," said William, "come round here."

He led him round to a garage at the back of the house and opened the door.

The garage was full of mixed infants having the time of their lives, engaged in mimic warfare under the leadership of Ginger and Douglas with ammunition of tea-leaves and tobacco.

Certainly the mixed infants were appreciating the old folks' presents far more than the old folks had appreciated the mixed infants'.

"Here they are," said William carelessly,

"you can have 'em if you like. We're gettin' a bit tired of them."

No words of mine could describe the touching reunion between the mixed infants and their mothers.

Neither could any words of mine describe the first practice of Mr Solomon's Sunday school band with William, Ginger, Henry and Douglas as trumpeters.

There was, however, only one practice, as after that Mr Solomon wisely decided to go away for a very long holiday.

William's New Year's Day

Mr Moss, who owned the village sweet-shop, handed a fruit drop to William. William received it gratefully.

"An' what good resolution are you going to take tomorrow?" said Mr Moss.

William crunched in silence for a minute, then, "Good resolution?" he questioned. "I ain't got none."

"You've got to have a good resolution for New Year's Day," said Mr Moss firmly.

William pondered.

"Can't think of anything," he said. "You think of somethin' for me."

"Well, you might take one to do your schoolwork properly."

William shook his head very firmly.

"Crumbs, no!"

"Or to be polite."

"P'lite?"

"Yes. 'Please' and 'thank you', and 'if you don't mind me sayin' so', and 'if you excuse me contradictin' of you', and 'can I do anything for you?' and such like."

William was struck with this.

"Yes, I might be that," he said. "Yes, I might try bein' that. How long has it to go on, though?"

"Not long," said Mr Moss. "Only the first day gen'rally. Folks gen'rally give 'em up after that."

"What's yours?" said William.

Mr Moss leant forward confidentially.

"I'm goin' to arsk 'er again," he said.

"Who?" said William, mystified.

"Someone I've arsked reg'lar every New Year's Day for ten year."

"Asked what?"

"Arsked to take me, o' course,"

"Take you where? Where d'you want to go?
Why can't you go yourself?"

"Ter *marry* me, I means," said Mr Moss,
blushing slightly as he spoke.

"Well," said William with a judicial air, "I
wun't have asked the same one for ten years.
I'd have tried someone else. You'd be sure to
find someone that wouldn't mind you – with
a sweet-shop, too. She must be a softie. Does
she *know* you've got a sweet-shop?"

*

The next morning William leapt out of bed with an expression of stern resolve.

"I'm goin' to be p'lite," he remarked to his bedroom furniture. "I'm goin' to be p'lite all day."

He met his father on the stairs.

"Good mornin', Father," he said. "Can I do anythin' for you today?"

His father looked down at him suspiciously.

"What do you want now?" he demanded.

William was hurt.

"I'm only bein' p'lite. It's – you know – one of those things you take on New Year's Day. Well, I've took one to be p'lite."

His father apologised.

"I'm sorry. You see, I'm not used to it. It startled me."

After breakfast, William made his way to the sweet-shop.

Mr Moss was at the door, hatted and coated, and gazing anxiously down the street.

"Goo' mornin', Mr Moss," said William politely.

Mr Moss took out a large antique watch.

"He's late!" he said. "I shall miss the train. Oh, dear! It will be the first New Year's Day I've missed in ten years. Will you – will you do something for me and I'll *give* you a quarter of those new pink ones."

William gasped. The offer was almost too munificent to be true.

"I'll do *anythin'* for that," he said simply.

"Well, just stay in the shop till my nephew Bill comes. 'E'll be 'ere in two shakes, an' I'll miss my train if I don't go now. 'E's goin' to keep the shop for me till I'm back. You can weigh yourself a quarter o' those sweets."

William was left alone. The ideal of his childhood was realised. He had a sweet-shop.

He walked round the shop with a conscious swagger, pausing to pop a butter-ball into his mouth.

It was all his – all those rows and rows of

gleaming bottles of sweets of every size and colour, those boxes and boxes of attractively arranged chocolates.

He owned them all.

A small boy appeared in the doorway. William scowled at him.

"Well," he said ungraciously, "what d'you want?"

Then, suddenly remembering his Resolution, "*Please* what d'you want?"

"Where's Uncle?" said the small boy with equal ungraciousness. "'Cause our Bill's ill, an' can't come."

William waved him off.

"That's all right," he said. "You tell 'em that's all right. That's quite all right. See? Now, you go off!"

The small boy stood, as though rooted to the spot. William pressed into one of his hands a stick of liquorice and into the other a packet of chocolate.

"Now, you go *away*! I don't *want* you here. See?"

The small boy made off, clutching his spoils.

William called after the retreating figure, "If you don't mind me sayin' so."

He had already come to look upon the New Year's Resolution as a kind of god who must at all costs be propitiated.

Already the Resolution seemed to have bestowed upon him the dream of his life – a fully equipped sweet-shop.

A thin lady of uncertain age came in.

"Good morning," she said icily. "Where's Mr Moss?"

William answered as well as the presence of five sweets in his mouth would allow him.

"Gone," he said, then murmured vaguely, "thank you," as the thought of the Resolution loomed up in his mind.

"Who's in charge?"

"Me," said William.

She looked at him with distinct disapproval.

"Well, I'll have one of those bars of chocolate."

William, looking round the shop, realised suddenly there was a chance of making good any loss that Mr Moss might otherwise have sustained.

He looked down at the twopenny bars.

"Shillin' each," he said firmly.

She gasped.

"They were only twopence yesterday."

"They're gone up since, if you'll kin'ly 'scuse me sayin' so."

"Gone up—? Have you heard from the makers they're gone up?"

"Yes'm," said William politely.

"When did you hear?"

"This mornin' if you don't mind me sayin' so."

William's manner of fulsome politeness seemed to madden her.

"Did you hear by post?"

"Yes'm. By post this mornin'."

She glared at him with vindictive triumph.

"I happen to live opposite, you wicked lying boy, and I know that the postman did not call here this morning."

William met her eye calmly.

"No, they came round to see me in the night – the makers did. You cou'n't of heard them," he added hastily. "It was when you was asleep. If you'll 'scuse me contradictin' of you."

It is a great gift to be able to lie so as to convince other people. It is a still greater gift to be able to lie so as to convince yourself.

73

William was possessed of the latter gift.

"I shall certainly not pay more than twopence," said his customer severely, taking a bar of chocolate and laying down twopence on the counter. "And I shall report this shop to the Profiteering Committee. It's scandalous."

William scowled at her.

"They're a *shillin'*," he said. "I don't want your nasty ole tuppences. I said they was a *shillin'*."

He followed her to the door. She was crossing the street to her house. "You – you ole *thief*!" he yelled after her, though, true to his Resolution, he added softly with dogged determination, "if you don't mind me sayin' so."

He was next disturbed by the entry of another customer. Swallowing a nutty football whole, he hastened to his post behind the counter.

The newcomer was a dainty little girl of about nine – dressed in a white fur coat and cap and long white gaiters.

William had seen this vision on various occasions in the town, but had never yet addressed it.

He smiled – a self-conscious, sheepish smile – as she came up to the counter.

"Please, I want two twopenny bars of chocolate."

She laid four pennies on the counter.

"You can have lots for that," said William huskily. "An' – what else would you like?"

"Please, I haven't any more money," gasped a small, bewildered voice.

"*Money* don't matter," said William. "Things is cheap today. You can have – anythin' you like for that fourpence. Anythin' you like."

"'Cause it's New Year's Day?" said the vision, with a gleam of understanding.

"Yes," said William, "'cause it's that."

"Is it your shop?"

"Yes," said William with an air of importance. "It's all my shop. You take anythin' you like."

She collected as much as she could carry and started towards the door. "*Sank* you! Sank you ever so!" she said gratefully.

"It's all right," said William with an indulgent smile. "Not at all. Don't menshun it. Not at all. Quite all right."

He bowed with would-be gracefulness as she went through the doorway.

As she passed the window, she stopped and kissed her hand.

William blinked with pure emotion.

Then, absent-mindedly, crammed his mouth with a handful of mixed dewdrops.

As he crunched he caught sight of two of his friends flattening their noses at the window. He went to the door.

They gazed at him in wonder.

"I've got a shop," he said casually. "Come on in an' look at it."

They entered, open-mouthed. They gazed at the boxes and bottles of sweets. Aladdin's Cave was nothing to this.

"How'd you get it, William?" gasped Ginger.

"Someone gave it me," said William. "I took one of them things to be p'lite, and someone gave it to me. Go on, jus' help yourselves. Not at all. Jus' help yourselves an' don't menshun it."

They needed no second bidding.

They went from box to box, putting handfuls of sweets and chocolates into their mouths. They said nothing, because speech was a physical impossibility.

A close observer might have noticed that William now ate little.

William himself had been conscious for some time of a curious and inexplicable feeling of coldness towards the tempting dainties around him.

He was, however, loath to give in to the weakness, and every now and then he nonchalantly put into his mouth a toasted square or a fruity bit.

It happened that a loutish boy of about

fourteen was passing the shop. At the sight of three small boys rapidly consuming the contents, he became interested.

"What yer doin'?" he said indignantly, standing in the doorway.

"You get out of my shop," said William valiantly.

"*Yer* shop?" said the boy. "Yer bloomin' well pinchin' things out o' someone else's shop. 'Ere, gimme some of them."

"You get *out*!" said William.

"Get out *yerself*!" said the other.

"If I'd not took one to be p'lite," said William threateningly, "I'd knock you down."

"Yer would, would yer?" said the other, beginning to roll up his sleeves.

"Yes, I would, too. You get out."

Seizing the nearest bottle, which happened to contain acid drops, William began to fire them at his opponent's head. One hit him in the eye. He retired into the street. William followed him, still hurling acid drops with all his might.

A crowd of boys collected together. Some gathered acid drops from the gutter, others joined the scrimmage.

William, Henry and Ginger carried on a noble fight against heavy odds.

It was only the sight of the proprietor of the shop coming briskly down the sidewalk that put an end to the battle.

The street boys made off in one direction and Ginger and Henry in another. William, clasping an empty acid drop bottle to his bosom, was left to face Mr Moss.

Mr Moss entered and looked round with an air of bewilderment.

"Where's Bill?" he said.

"He's ill," said William. "He couldn't come. I've been keepin' shop for you. I've done the best I could."

He looked round the rifled shop anxiously. But Mr Moss hardly seemed to notice.

"Thanks, William," he said almost humbly. "William, she's took me. She's goin' ter marry me. Isn't it grand? After all these years."

"I'm afraid there's a bit of a mess," said William.

Mr Moss waved aside his apologies.

"It doesn't matter, William," he said. "Nothing matters today. She's took me at last. I'm goin' to shut shop this afternoon and go over to her again. Thanks for staying, William."

"Not at all. Don't menshun it," said William nobly. Then, "I think I've had enough of that bein' p'lite. Will one mornin' do for this year, d'you think?"

"Er – yes. Well, I'll shut up. Don't you stay, William. You'll want to be getting home for lunch."

Lunch? Quite definitely William decided that he did not want any lunch.

The very thought of lunch brought with it a feeling of active physical discomfort, which was much more than mere absence of hunger.

He decided to go home as quickly as possible, though not to lunch.

"Goo'bye," he said.

"Goodbye," said Mr Moss.

"I'm afraid you'll find some things gone," said William faintly. "Some boys was in."

"That's all right, William," said Mr Moss, roused again from his rosy dreams. "That's quite all right."

But it was not "quite all right" with William.

If you had been left, at the age of eleven, in sole charge of a sweet-shop for a whole morning, would it have been "all right" with you? No.

But we will not follow William through the humiliating hours of the afternoon. We will leave him pale and unsteady, but for now master of the situation, as he wends his homeward way.

William's Haunted House

and Other Stories

Contents

William's Haunted House

The Outlaws had discovered that the old house next door to Miss Hatherly was empty.

"I say," said William, "it'd be just the place for a meeting-place, wun't it? Better than the old barn."

"Yes, but we'd have to be quieter," said Ginger, "or else people'll be hearin' us an' makin' a fuss like what they always do."

William knew Miss Hatherly, whose house overlooked the empty house. He had good cause to know her.

Robert (William's grown-up brother) was deeply enamoured of Marion, Miss Hatherly's niece, and Miss Hatherly disapproved of Robert because he had no money and rode a very noisy motorcycle and dropped cigarette ash on her carpets.

She disapproved of William still more and for reasons too numerous to state.

The empty house became the regular meeting-place of the Outlaws. They always entered cautiously by a hole in the garden hedge, first looking up and down the road to be sure that no one saw them.

The house served many purposes besides that of meeting-place. It was a smuggler's den, a castle, a desert island, and an Indian camp.

It was William, of course, who suggested the midnight feast and the idea was received with eager joy by the others. The next night they all got up and dressed when the rest of their households were in bed.

Cautiously, they made their way to the old house and entered it – disturbing several rats who fled at their approach.

They sat around a stubby candle-end thoughtfully provided by Henry.

They ate sardines and buns and cheese and jam and cakes and desiccated coconut on the dusty floor in the empty upstairs room whose paper hung in cobwebby strands from the wall, while rats squeaked indignantly behind the wainscotting, and the moon, pale with surprise, peeped in at the dirty uncurtained window.

They munched in happy silence and drank lemonade and liquorice-water provided by William.

"I say, let's do it tomorrow, too," said Henry as they rose to depart, and the proposal was eagerly agreed to.

Miss Hatherly was a member of the Society for the Encouragement of Higher Thought. The Society for the Encouragement of Higher Thought had exhausted nearly every branch of Higher Thought. But last week someone had suggested Psychical Revelation.

"We must all collect data," said the President brightly.

"What's 'data'?" said little Miss Simky to her neighbour in a mystified whisper.

"It's French for ghost story," said Miss Sluker.

"Oh!" said little Miss Simky, satisfied.

The next meeting was at Miss Hatherly's house.

The "data" were not very extensive.

"I'm afraid I've no personal experience to record," said little Miss Simky, "though I've

92

read some very exciting datas in magazines and such like – but I'm afraid they won't count."

Then Miss Hatherly, trembling with eagerness, spoke.

"I have a very important revelation to make," she said. "I have discovered that Colonel Henks's old house is haunted."

There was a breathless silence. The eyes of the members of the Society for the Encouragement of Higher Thought almost fell through their spectacles on to the floor.

"*Haunted!*" they screamed in chorus, and little Miss Simky clung to her neighbour in terror.

"Listen!" said Miss Hatherly. "The house is empty, yet I have heard voices and footsteps – the footsteps resembling Colonel Henks's. Last night," – the round-eyed, round-mouthed circle drew nearer – "last night, I heard them most distinctly at midnight, and I firmly believe that Colonel Henks's spirit is trying to attract my attention. I believe that he has a message for me."

Little Miss Simky gave a shrill scream.

"Tonight I shall go there," said Miss Hatherly, and the seekers after Higher Thought screamed again.

"I shall go tonight," she repeated, "and I shall receive the message. I want you all to meet me here this time tomorrow and I will report my experience."

"Oh – what a thrilling data it will make," breathed little Miss Simky.

William was creeping downstairs. It was too windy for him to use the pear tree that grew right up to his bedroom window.

He was dressed in an overcoat over his pyjamas, and he held in his arms ten small apples which were his contribution to the feast.

He looked round anxiously. His arms seemed inadequate for ten apples, but he had promised ten apples for the feast and he must provide them. His pockets were already full of biscuits.

He looked round the moonlit hall. Ah, Robert's "overflow bag"! It was on one of the chairs. Robert had been staying with a friend and had returned late that night.

He had taken his suitcase upstairs and flung the small and shabby bag that he called his "overflow bag" down on a chair. It was still there.

Good! It would do to hold the apples. William opened it. There were a few things inside, but William couldn't stay to take them out. There was plenty of room for the apples anyway.

He shoved them in, took up the bag, and made his way to the dining-room window.

The midnight feast was in full swing.

Henry had forgotten to bring candles, Douglas was half asleep, Ginger was racked by gnawing internal pains as the result of the feast of the night before, and William's mind was on other things; but otherwise all was well.

Someone had given William an old camera the day before and his thoughts were full of it. He had taken six snapshots and was going to develop them tomorrow. He had sold his bow and arrows to a class-mate to buy the necessary chemicals.

As he munched the apples and cheesecakes and chocolate cream and pickled onions and currants provided for the feast, he was, in imagination, developing and fixing his snapshots.

He'd never done it before. He thought he'd enjoy it. It would be so jolly and messy – watery stuff to slosh about in little basins and that kind of thing.

Suddenly, as they munched and lazily discussed the rival merits of catapults and bows and arrows, there came through the silent empty house the sound of the opening of the front door.

The Outlaws stared at each other with crumby mouths wide open – steps were now ascending the front stairs.

Suddenly, a loud and vibrant voice called from the middle of the stairs, "Speak!"

It made the Outlaws start almost out of their skins.

"Speak! Give me your message."

The hair of the Outlaws stood on end.

"A ghost!" whispered Henry with chattering teeth.

"Crikey!" said William. "Let's get out."

They crept silently out of the further door, down the back stairs, out of the window, and fled with all their might down the road.

Meanwhile, upstairs, Miss Hatherly first walked majestically into the closed door and then fell over Robert's "overflow bag" which the Outlaws had forgotten in their panic.

Robert went to see his beloved Marion next day to reassure her of his undying affection. She yawned several times in the course of his speech. She was beginning to find Robert's devotion somewhat monotonous.

"I say," she said, interrupting him as he was telling her that he'd made up a lot more poetry about her but had forgotten to bring it, "do come indoors. They're having some sort of stunt in the drawing-room – Aunt and the High Thinkers, you know. I'm not quite sure what it is – something psychic, she said, but anyway, it ought to be amusing."

Rather reluctantly, Robert followed her into the drawing-room where the Higher Thinkers were assembled. The Higher

Thinkers looked coldly at Robert. He wasn't much thought of in high-thinking circles.

There was an air of intense excitement in the room as Miss Hatherly rose to speak.

"I entered the haunted house," she began in a low, quivering voice, "and at once I heard – *voices*!"

Miss Simky clung in panic to Miss Sluker.

"I proceeded up the stairs and I heard – *footsteps*! I went on undaunted—"

The Higher Thinkers gave a thrilled murmur of admiration.

"And suddenly all was silent, but I felt a – *presence*! It led me – led me along a passage – I *felt* it! It led me to a room—"

Miss Simky screamed again.

"And in the room I found *this*!"

With a dramatic gesture, she brought out Robert's "overflow bag".

"I have not yet investigated it. I wished to do so first in your presence. I feel sure that this is what Colonel Henks has been trying to show me. I am convinced that this will throw light upon the mystery of his death – I am now going to open it."

"If it's human remains," quavered Miss Simky, "I shall faint."

With a determined look, Miss Hatherly opened the bag.

From it she brought out first a pair of faded and very much darned blue socks; next a shirt with a large hole in it; next a bathing suit; and lastly a pair of very grimy white flannel trousers.

The Higher Thinkers looked bewildered. But Miss Hatherly was not daunted.

"They're clues!" she said. "Clues – they must have some meaning. Ah, here's a notebook – this will explain everything."

She opened the notebook and began to read aloud:

"Oh, Marion, my lady fair,
Has eyes of blue and golden hair.
Her heart of gold is kind and true,
She is the sweetest girl you ever knew.
But oh, a dragon guards this jewel,
A hideous dragon, foul and cruel.
The ugliest old thing you ever did see,
Is Marion's aunt, Miss Hatherly—
     What?"*

"These socks are both marked 'Robert Brown'," suddenly cried Miss Sluker, who had been examining the "clues".

Miss Hatherly gave a scream of rage and turned to the corner where Robert had been.

But Robert had vanished.

When Robert saw his "overflow bag" he had turned red.

When he saw his socks he had turned purple.

When he saw his shirt he had turned green.

When he saw his trousers he had turned white.

When he saw his notebook he had turned yellow.

When Miss Hatherly began to read he had muttered something about feeling faint and crept unostentatiously out of the window. Marion followed him.

"Well," she said sternly, "you've made a nice mess of everything, haven't you? What on earth have you been doing?"

"I can't think what you thought of those old clothes," said Robert. "I never wear them. I don't know why they were in the bag."

"Oh, do shut up about your things," snapped Marion. "I don't care what you wear. But I'm sick with your writing soppy poetry about me for those asses to read. And why did you give her your bag, you loony?"

"I didn't, Marion," said Robert miserably. "It's a mystery to me how she got it. I've been hunting for it high and low all today. It's simply a mystery!"

"Oh, do stop saying that. What are you going to do about it? That's the point."

"I'm going to commit suicide," said Robert. "I feel there's nothing left to live for now you're turning against me."

"I don't believe you could," said Marion aggressively. "How are you going to do it?"

"I shall drink poison."

"What poison? I don't believe you know what are poisons. What poison?"

"Er – prussic acid," said Robert.

"You couldn't get it. They wouldn't sell it to you."

"People do get poisons," Robert said indignantly. "I'm always reading of people taking poisons."

They had reached Robert's house and were standing just beneath William's window.

"I know heaps of poisons," said Robert. "I'm not going to tell you what I'm going to take. I'm going to—"

At that moment, William, who had been fixing his snapshots and was beginning to "clear up", threw the contents of his fixing bath out of the window with a careless flourish. They fell upon Robert and Marion. For a minute they were both speechless with surprise and solution of sodium hydrosulphate. Then Marion said furiously, "You brute! I hate you."

"Oh, I say," gasped Robert. "It's not my fault, Marion. I don't know what it is. Honestly, I didn't do it—"

Some of the solution had found its way into Robert's mouth and he was trying to eject it as politely as possible.

"It came from your beastly house," said Marion angrily, "and it's ruined my hat and I hate you and I'll never speak to you again."

She turned on her heel and walked off, mopping the back of her neck with a handkerchief as she went.

Robert stared at her unrelenting back till she was out of sight, then went indoors. Ruined her hat indeed? What was a hat anyway? It had ruined his suit – simply ruined it. And how had the old cat got his bag he'd like to know. He wouldn't mind betting a quid that that little wretch William had had something to do with it. He always had.

He decided not to commit suicide after all. He decided to live for years and years and years to make the little wretch's life a misery to him – if he could!

William's Truthful Christmas

William went to church with his family every Sunday morning, but he did not usually listen to the sermon.

But this Sunday, attracted by the frequent repetition of the word "Christmas", William put his stag-beetle back into its box and gave his whole attention to the Vicar's exhortation . . .

"What is it that poisons our whole social life?" said the Vicar earnestly. "What is it that spoils even the holy season that lies before us? It is untruthfulness. Let each one of us decide here and now, for this season of

Christmas at least, to cast aside all deceit and hypocrisy, and speak the truth one with another . . . It will be the first step to a holier life. It will make this Christmas the happiest of our lives . . ."

These words made a deep impression on William. He decided (for this holy season at least) to cast aside deceit and hypocrisy and speak the truth one with another.

He decided to try it at Christmas as the Vicar had suggested.

Much to his disgust William heard that Uncle Frederick and Aunt Emma had asked his family to stay with them for Christmas.

It happened that William's father was summoned on Christmas Eve to the sickbed of one of his aunts and so could not accompany them.

Uncle Frederick and Aunt Emma were very stout and good-natured-looking. They had not seen William since he was a baby.

That explained the fact of their having invited William and his family to spend

Christmas with them.

"So this is little William," said Uncle Frederick, putting his hand on William's head. "And how is little William?"

William removed his head from Uncle Frederick's hand in silence, then said, "V'well, thank you."

"And so grateful to your uncle and aunt for asking you to stay with them, aren't you, William?" said his mother.

William remembered that his career of

truthfulness did not begin till the next day, so he said, "Yes . . ."

William awoke early on Christmas Day. He had hung up his stocking the night before and was pleased to see it fairly full. He took out the presents quickly but not very optimistically.

Yes, as bad as ever! . . . A case containing a pen and pencil and ruler, a new brush and comb, a purse (empty) and a new tie . . . A penknife and a box of toffee were the only redeeming features.

On the chair by his bedside was a book of Church History from Aunt Emma and a box containing a pair of compasses, a protractor and a set square from Uncle Frederick . . .

William appeared at breakfast carrying under his arm his presents for his host and hostess. He exchanged "Happy Christmas" gloomily.

His resolve to cast away deceit and

hypocrisy and speak the truth one with another lay heavy upon him.

"Well, William, darling," said his mother, "did you find your presents?"

"Yes. Thank you."

"Did you like the book and instruments that Uncle and I gave you?" said Aunt Emma brightly.

"No," said William truthfully. "I'm not int'rested in Church History, an' I've got something like those at school. Not that I'd want 'em, if I *hadn't* 'em."

"*William!*" screamed Mrs Brown in horror. "How can you be so ungrateful!"

"I'm not ungrateful," explained William. "I'm only bein' truthful. I'm casting aside deceit an' . . . an' hyp-hyp— what he said. I'm only sayin' that I'm not int'rested in Church History nor in those inst'ments. But thank you very much for 'em."

There was a horrified silence during which William drew his paper packages from under his arm.

"Here are your Christmas presents from me," he said.

The atmosphere brightened.

"It's very kind of you," said Aunt Emma, struggling with the string.

"It's not kind," said William, still treading doggedly the path of truth. "Mother said I'd got to bring you something."

Mrs Brown coughed suddenly and loudly.

"But still – er – very kind," said Aunt Emma, though with less enthusiasm.

At last she brought out a small pincushion.

"Thank you very much, William. You really oughtn't to have spent your money on me like this."

"I din't," said William stonily. "It was left over from Mother's stall at the fête an' Mother said it was no use keepin' it for nex' year because it had got so faded."

Again Mrs Brown coughed loudly but too late. Aunt Emma said, "I see. Yes. Your mother was quite right. But thank you all the same, William."

Uncle Frederick was holding up a leather purse.

"Ah, this is a really useful present," he said jovially.

"I'm 'fraid it's not," said William. "Uncle Jim sent it to Father for his birthday, but Father said it was no use 'cause the catch wouldn' catch, so he gave it to me to give to you."

As soon as the Brown family were left alone it turned upon William in a combined attack.

"I *warned* you!" said Ethel to her mother.

"He ought to be hung," said Robert.

"William, how *could* you?" said Mrs Brown.

During the afternoon there came the sound of a car drawing up. Uncle Frederick looked out of the window.

"It's Lady Atkinson," he said. "Help! Help!"

"Now, Frederick dear," said Aunt Emma hastily. "Don't talk like that and *do* try to be nice to her. She's one of *the* Atkinsons, you know," she explained to Mrs Brown in a whisper as the lady was shown in.

Lady Atkinson was stout and elderly and wore a very youthful hat and coat.

"A happy Christmas to you all!" she said graciously. "The boy? Your nephew? William? How do you do, William?"

She greeted everyone with infinite condescension.

"I've brought you my Christmas present in person," she went on. "Look!"

She took out of an envelope a large signed

photograph of herself. "There now . . . What do you think of that?

Murmurs of admiration and gratitude.

"It's very good, isn't it? You – little boy – don't you think it's very like me?"

William gazed at it critically.

"It's not as fat as you are," was his final offering at the altar of truth.

"*William!*" screamed Mrs Brown. "How *can* you be so impolite!"

"Impolite?" said William. "I'm bein' *truthful*. I can't be everything. Seems to me I'm the only person in the world what *is* truthful an' no one seems to be grateful to me. It *isn't* 's fat as what she is," he went on doggedly, "an' it's not got as many little lines on its face as what she has, an' it's different lookin' altogether. It looks pretty an' she doesn't—"

Lady Atkinson towered over him, quivering with rage. "You *nasty* little boy! You – NASTY – little – boy!"

She swept out of the room.

The front door slammed.

William's family were speechless with horror.

Aunt Emma began to weep. "She'll never come to the house again."

"I don't think she will, my dear," said Uncle Frederick cheerfully. "Nothing like the truth, William . . . absolutely nothing."

A diversion was caused at this moment by the arrival of the post. Among it there was a

Christmas card from an artist who had a studio about five minutes' walk from the house.

"How kind of him!" Aunt Emma said. "And we never sent him anything. But there's that calendar that Mr Franks sent to us and it's not written on. Perhaps William could be trusted to take it to Mr Fairly with our compliments while the rest of us go for a short walk."

William was glad of an excuse for escaping. He set off and finally arrived at Mr Fairly's studio. William handed the calendar to Mr Fairly who opened the door. Mr Fairly showed him into the studio with a low bow.

Mr Fairly had a pointed beard and a theatrical manner. He had obviously lunched well – as far as liquid refreshment was concerned at any rate. He was moved to tears by the calendar.

"How kind! How very kind. My dear young friend, forgive this emotion. The world is hard. I am not used to kindness. If you will excuse me, my dear young friend, I will retire to my bedroom where I have the wherewithal to write a letter of thanks to your most delightful and charming relative. I beg you to make yourself at home here . . . Use my house, my dear young friend, as though it were your own . . ."

He waved his arms and retreated unsteadily to an inner room, closing the door behind him.

William sat down and waited. Suddenly a fresh aspect of his Christmas resolution occurred to him.

If you were speaking the truth one with another yourself, surely you might take everything that other people said for truth?

He'd said, "Use this house, my dear young friend, as though it were your own . . ." Well, he would.

William went across the room and opened a cupboard. It contained a medley of paints, two palettes and a cake.

He attacked the cake with gusto. William felt refreshed. He looked round the studio: a figure sat upon a couch on a small platform.

William approached it cautiously. It was almost life-size, like a large puppet, and clad in a piece of thin silk.

William lifted it. It was quite light. He put it on a chair by the window.

Then he dressed the figure in a bonnet and mackintosh he saw hanging on a peg. He found a piece of black gauze and put it over the figure's face as a veil, and tied it round the bonnet.

He felt all the thrill of a creative artist. He shook hands with it and talked to it. He called it Annabel.

Then he remembered the note he was waiting for. He knocked gently at the bedroom door. There was no answer. He opened the door and entered. On the writing-table by the door was a letter:

Dear Friend,
Many thanks for your beautiful calendar.
Words fail me . . .

Then came a blot and that was all. Words had failed Mr Fairly so completely that he lay outstretched on the sofa by the window, sleeping the sleep of the slightly inebriated. William returned to the studio.

Then he thought of a game. He caught up the figure in his arms and dashed into the street with it. The danger and exhilaration of this race for freedom through the street with

Annabel in his arms was too enticing to be resisted.

As a matter of fact the flight through the streets was rather disappointing. He met no one, and no one pursued him.

He staggered up the steps to Aunt Emma's house still carrying Annabel. There he realised that his rescue of Annabel was not likely to be received enthusiastically by his home circle. And Annabel was not easy to conceal.

The house seemed empty, but he could already hear them returning from their walk.

The drawing-room door was open, and into it he rushed, deposited Annabel in a chair by the fireplace with her back to the door, and returned to the hall. He assumed his most vacant expression.

To his surprise they crept past the drawing-room door on tiptoe and congregated in the dining-room.

"A caller," said Aunt Emma. "Did you see?"

"Yes, in the drawing-room," said Mrs Brown. "I saw her hat through the window."

"Curses!" said Uncle Frederick. "The maids must have shown her in before they went up to change."

"Perhaps she's collecting for something," said Mrs Brown.

William stood at the back of the group with a sphinx-like expression.

They all crept into the hall. Uncle Frederick went just inside the drawing-room and coughed loudly. Annabel did not move. "Good afternoon," he bellowed.

Annabel still did not move. He went up to her.

"Now look here, my woman—" he began.

But at that instant Mr Fairly burst into the house like a whirlwind, still slightly inebriated and screaming with rage.

"Where's the thief? Where is he? He's stolen my figure. He's eaten my tea. Where is he? He's stolen my charwoman's clothes. He's stolen my figure. He's eaten my tea. Wait till I get him!"

He caught sight of Annabel, rushed into the drawing-room, caught her up in his arms and turned round upon the circle of open-mouthed spectators.

"I *hate* you!" he screamed. "And your nasty little calendars and your nasty little boys!"

With a final snort of fury he turned, still clasping Annabel, and staggered down the front steps. Speechless, they watched his departure. Then, no longer speechless, they turned on William.

"William," said Mrs Brown, "I don't know what's happened and I don't *want* to know but I shall tell your father *all* about it *directly* we get home."

Uncle Frederick saw them off at the station the next day. He slipped a half-crown into William's hand.

"Buy yourself something with that. I'm really grateful to you about Lady— Well, I think Emma's right. I don't think she'll ever come again."

That evening, his father's question as to whether William had been good had been answered as usual in the negative and, refusing to listen to details of accusation or defence, he docked William a month's pocket-money.

But William was not depressed. The ordeal of Christmas was over. Normal life stretched before him once more. His spirits rose. He wandered out into the lane.

There he met Ginger. From Ginger's face,

too, a certain gloom cleared as he saw William.

"Well," said William, "'v you enjoyed it?"

"I had a pair of braces from my aunt," said Ginger. "A pair of *braces*!"

William's grievances burst out.

"I went to church an' took what the Vicar said an' I've been speaking the truth one with another an' leadin' a holier life an' well, it jolly well din't make it the happiest Christmas of my life like what he said it would . . . It

made it the worst. Everyone mad at me all the time – I think I was the only person in the world speaking the truth one with another. And they've took off my pocket-money for it. Well, I've done with it. I'm going back to deceit and – and – oh, what's that word beginning with 'hyp'?"

"Hypnotism?" suggested Ginger.

"Yes, that's it," said William. "Well, I'm goin' back to it first thing tomorrow mornin'."

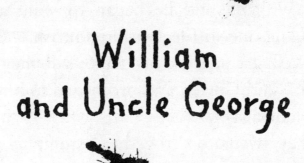

William and Uncle George

It was William who bought the horn-rimmed spectacles.

He bought them for sixpence from a boy who had bought them for a shilling from a boy to whose dead aunt's cousin's grandfather they had belonged.

William was intensely proud of them. He wore them in school all the morning. They made everything look vague and blurred, but he bore that inconvenience gladly for the sake of the prestige they lent him.

He was wearing them now as he and Ginger walked home from school.

"I can walk like a man with a false leg," said William, and he began to walk along swinging one stiff leg with a flourish.

"Well, I can click my teeth 's if they was false," said Ginger, and proceeded to bite the air vigorously.

They went on together, stumping and clicking with great determination. Suddenly, they both stopped.

On the footpath just outside a door that opened straight on to the street, stood a bath chair. In it were a rug and a scarf.

"Ah! Here's my bath chair," said William. "'S tirin' walkin' like this with a false leg all the time."

He sat down in the chair. The sensation of being the possessor of both horn-rimmed spectacles and a false leg had been a proud and happy one. He wrapped the rug around his knees.

"You'd better push me a bit," he said to Ginger.

Ginger began to push the bath chair, at first

reluctantly but finally warming to his task. He tore along at a breakneck speed.

William held the precious horn-rimmed spectacles in place with one hand and with the other clutched on to the side of the chair. They stopped for breath at the end of the street.

"You're a jolly good pusher!" said William.

He tucked in his rug and adjusted his spectacles again.

"Do I look like a pore old man?" he said proudly.

Ginger gave a scornful laugh.

"No, you don't. You've gotta boy's face. You've got no lines or whiskers or screwedupness like an old man."

William drew his mouth down and screwed up his eyes into a hideous contortion.

"Do I now?" he said.

Ginger looked at him dispassionately.

"You look like a kind of monkey now," he said.

William took the long knitted scarf that was at the bottom of the bath chair and wound it round his head and face till only his horn-rimmed spectacles could be seen.

"Do I now?" he said in a muffled voice.

"Yes, you do now. At least you look 's if you might be *anything* now."

"All right," said William in his faraway muffled voice. "Pretend I'm an old man. Wheel me back now . . . *slowly*, mind! 'Cause I'm an old man."

They began the return journey. William leant back feebly in his chair enjoying the role of aged invalid, his horn-rimmed spectacles peering out with an air of deep wisdom from a waste of woollen muffler.

Suddenly a woman who was passing stopped.

"Uncle George!" she said in a tone of welcome and surprise.

She was tall and thin and gaily dressed.

"Well, this *is* a pleasant surprise," she said. "When you didn't answer our letter we thought you really weren't going to come to see us. And now I find you on your way to our house. *What* a treat for us! I'd have known you anywhere, *dear* Uncle George, even if I hadn't recognised the bath chair, and the muffler that I knitted for you on your last birthday."

She dropped a vague kiss upon the woollen muffler and then turned to Ginger.

"This boy can go. I can take you on to the house."

She slipped a coin into Ginger's hand.

"Now run away, little boy! I'll look after him."

Ginger, after one bewildered look, fled, and the lady began to push William's chair along briskly.

She bent down and shouted in his ear.

"And how *are* you, dear Uncle George?"

William looked desperately round for some chance of escape, but saw none. Feeling that some reply was necessary, and not wishing to let his voice betray him, he growled.

"So glad," yelled the tall lady into the muffler, "so glad. If you *think* you're better, you *will* be better, you know, as I always used to tell you."

To his horror, William saw that he was being taken in through a large gateway and up a drive. He felt as though he had been captured by some terrible enemy.

He couldn't breathe, and he could hardly see, and he didn't know what was going to happen to him. He growled again.

She left him on a small lawn and went through an opening in the box hedge. William could hear her talking to some people on the other side.

"He's *come*! Uncle George's *come*!" she said in a penetrating whisper.

"Oh *dear*!" said another voice. "He's *so* trying! What shall we do, Frederica?"

"He's *wealthy*, Mother. Anyway, we may as well try to placate him. He hasn't changed a bit, though he's dreadfully muffled up. And he's shrunk a little, I think – you know how old people do – and I'm afraid he's as touchy as ever."

"Perhaps you'd better explain to the boys, Frederica . . . ?"

"Oh *yes*! It's your Great-Uncle George, you know – *ever* so old, and we've not seen him for *ten* years, and he's just come to live here with his *male* attendant, you know, taken a furnished house, and though we asked him to come to see us – he's most *eccentric*, you know, simply won't see *anyone* at his own house – he never even answered and we thought he must be still annoyed. I told him the last time I saw him, ten years ago, that if only he'd think he could walk, he'd be *able* to walk, and it annoyed him. Anyway, to my surprise I found him on his *way* to our house this afternoon—"

William had almost decided to risk making a dash for it, when they all suddenly appeared through the opening in the hedge. William gave a gasp as he saw them.

First came Frederica, the tall, agile lady who had captured him; next a very old lady with a Roman nose and a pair of lorgnettes; next came a young curate; next a muscular young man in a college blazer; and last a little girl.

William knew the little girl. Her name was Emmeline, and she went to the same school as William – and William detested her.

His heart sank as they surrounded him. Nervously he pulled up his rug, spread out his muffler and crouched yet further down in his bath chair.

"You remember Mother, dear Uncle George, don't you?" screamed Frederica into the muffler.

The dignified dame raised the lorgnettes and held out a majestic hand. William merely growled. He was beginning to find the growl effective. They all hastily took a step back.

"Sulking!" explained Frederica in her penetrating whisper. "*Sulking!* Just because I told him on the way here that if he *willed* to be well he *would* be well."

"Hush, Frederica! He'll hear you!"

"No, dear, he's almost stone-deaf."

William growled again.

The old lady looked anxious. "I'm afraid he's ill. I hope it's nothing infectious! James, I think you'd better examine him."

Frederica drew one of the bashful and unwilling young men forward.

"This is your great-nephew, James," she shouted. "He's a MEDICAL STUDENT, and he'd SO love to talk to you."

The rest withdrew to the other end of the lawn and watched proceedings from a distance.

"Er – how are you, Uncle George?" said James politely. "If I could see your tongue – er – TONGUE – you seem to be in pain – perhaps – TONGUE – allow me."

He took hold of the muffler around William's head. William gave a sudden shake and a fierce growl and James started back as though he had been bitten.

William's growl was gaining a note of savage, almost blood-curdling ferocity. James

136

gazed at him apprehensively, then, as another growl began to arise from the depth of William's chair, hastily rejoined the others.

"I've – er – examined him," he said. "There's nothing – er – fundamentally wrong with him. He's just – er – got a foul temper, that's all."

"It is a case for you, then, I think, Jonathan," said the old lady grimly.

Frederica drew the reluctant curate across the lawn.

"This is your great-nephew, Jonathan," she yelled into the muffler. "He's in the CHURCH. He's looking forward SO much to a TALK with you, DEAR Uncle George."

With a sprightly nod at the horn-rimmed spectacles, she departed. Jonathan smiled mirthlessly. Then he proceeded to shout at William with whispered interjections.

"GOOD AFTERNOON, UNCLE GEORGE – confound you – WE'RE SO GLAD TO SEE YOU – don't think – WE EXPECT TO SEE A LOT OF YOU

NOW – worse luck – WE WANT TO BE A HAPPY UNITED FAMILY – you crusty old mummy – WE HOPE – er – WE HOPE – er—"

He stopped for breath. William, who was enjoying this part, chuckled. Jonathan, with a sigh of relief, departed.

"It's all right," he said airily. "The old chap's quite good-tempered now. My few words seemed to hit the spot."

William watched the group, wondering what was going to be done next and who was going to do it.

Then he saw two maids come round the house to the lawn.

One carried a table and the other a tray on which were some cakes that made William's mouth water, and – oh, scrummy! – there was a bowl of fruit salad.

Then to his horror he saw Emmeline being launched across the lawn to him by Frederica. Emmeline carried in her hand a bunch of roses. She laid them on the bath chair with an artless and confiding smile.

"Dear Great-Great-Uncle George," she said in her squeaky voice. "We're all so glad to see you and love you so much an'—"

The elders were watching the tableau with proud smiles, and William was summoning his breath for a really ferocious growl, when suddenly everyone turned round.

A little old man, purple with anger, had appeared, running up the drive.

"Where is he?" screamed the little old man

in fury. "They said he came in here – my bath chair – where is he? – the thief – the blackguard – how dare he? – I'll teach him – where is he?"

William did not wait to be taught. With admirable presence of mind he tore off his wrappings, flung away his horn-rimmed spectacles and dashed with all his might through the opening in the hedge and across the back lawn.

The little old man caught up a trowel that the gardener had left near a bed and flung it after William. It caught him neatly on the ankle and changed his swift flight to a limp.

"Dear Uncle George," cooed Frederica to the old man, "I don't know what's happened, but I *always* said you could walk quite well, if you liked."

With a howl of fury, the old man turned on her, snatched up the bowl of fruit salad and emptied it over her head—

The next day William met Ginger on the way to school.

140

"Well, *you're* brave, aren't you?" he said sarcastically, "goin' off an' leavin' me an not rescuin' me nor nothin'."

"I like that," said Ginger indignantly. "What could I do, I'd like to know. You *would* ride an' me push. 'F you'd bin unselfish an' pushed me, an' me rode, *you'd* 've got off."

Just then Emmeline appeared on the road, wearing the horn-rimmed spectacles.

"I say, those is ours!" said Ginger.

"Oh *no*!" said Emmeline with a shrill triumphant laugh. "I found them on our front lawn. They're *mine* now. You ask William Brown *how* I found them on our front lawn. But they're *mine* now. So there!"

For a moment William was nonplussed. Then a beatific smile spread over his freckled face.

"Dear Great-Great-Uncle George!" he mimicked in a shrill falsetto. "We're all so glad to see you – we love you so much."

Emmeline gave a howl of anger and ran

down the road holding her horn-rimmed spectacles on as she ran.

"I say, what happened yesterday?" said Ginger when she had disappeared.

"Oh, I can't quite remember," said William evasively. "I growled at 'em an' scared 'em no end an' I didn't get any tea an' he threw somethin' at me – oh, a lot of things like that – I can't quite remember. But I say" – with sudden interest – "how much did that woman give you?"

"Sixpence," said Ginger proudly, taking it out of his pocket.

"Come on!" said William joyfully. "Come on, an' let's spend it."

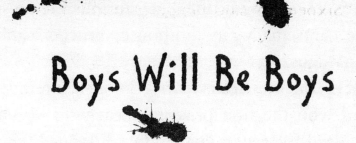

Boys Will Be Boys

William, much against his will, had been sent to stay with his Aunt Florence.

"I shall be very busy while you're here, William," she said. "I hope you'll be able to entertain yourself."

"Oh, yes," said William. "Oh, yes, I'll be able to entertain myself, all right."

The next morning he sallied forth to inspect the neighbourhood. It was a very small village.

Its chief interest and almost its only topic of conversation was the Flower Show that was to be held at the end of the month.

And that, mainly because of the rivalry of two old men. Of late their rivalry had crystallised into a furious contest for supremacy in hothouse peaches and asparagus.

For the last four years, Colonel Summers had won the first prize for peaches and Mr Foulard for asparagus, and each longed with all his heart and soul to beat the other in his speciality.

This year each had inwardly vowed to win the first prize for *both* . . .

All this William gathered in a stroll round the village.

One afternoon he ran violently into a man just entering a pair of impressive iron gates.

He found himself looking up into the yellow-moustached face of Colonel Summers.

"Well, well, well," said Colonel Summers. "I don't think I know your face, do I?"

"No," said William, scrambling to his feet. "I've come to stay with my aunt."

"Well! Well!" said the Colonel. "You'd better come in and have a brush down. You can't go back to your aunt in that state."

Nothing loath, William accompanied the tall figure up the drive and into the big white house at the end. The Colonel took a clothes brush from the hatstand and gave William a perfunctory brush down, then led him into a room hung round with various Eastern weapons.

"I dare say you'll be interested in these, my boy," he said, and proceeded to describe them in detail, with many somewhat lengthy anecdotes.

William was a most satisfactory audience. He listened open-mouthed. He examined the weapons with eager delight.

He was particularly interested in some Burmese knives in painted leather sheaths.

"Perhaps I'll give you one of those before you go," said Colonel Summers.

He was in high good humour. It was years since he had told the stories except to the accompaniment of strangled yawns. William was a godsend to him.

"Look in again some time," he said

genially, as he saw him off and pointed out a
short cut through the kitchen garden.

"And don't forget, I may give you one of
those knives before you go . . . Shut the gate
after you."

On his way to the gate, William passed a
large hothouse where the famous peaches
were ripening.

In the road he cannoned into someone else.
William became aware of the red, angry face
of Mr Foulard just above his own.

"I hope that'll teach you to look where you're going," he was saying as he administered a number of cuffs. "Disgraceful! Charging into people like that!"

Then he strutted angrily in at a gate that bore the inscription: "Uplands".

The next morning William called on Colonel Summers again. And the next. And the next.

William wanted the Burmese knife, and he shrewdly judged that he was expected to earn it by providing Colonel Summers with an audience.

One morning his footsteps lingered as he passed the hothouse. Today the door was open and the gardener absent . . .

William looked round. The temptation to go in and examine the peaches at closer quarters was irresistible. He went in.

He wouldn't dream of eating any. He stroked one softly.

At least he *meant* to stroke it softly, but to his consternation the stalk snapped and the peach fell on to the ground . . . He gazed at it, at first dismayed, then interested . . .

Well, he might as well *eat* it—

He sank his teeth into the soft flesh. It was *jolly* good. He'd never had anything quite so good.

He looked at the massed peaches all around him. They'd never miss just one more. Actually, he thought, there were far too many. It would be a kindness to thin these peaches a bit.

The best ones hung high overhead, but a ladder was conveniently set up against the top branch. He climbed up . . . took a peach and ate it . . . took another . . . and another . . .

Suddenly he heard a loud shout and the sound of running footsteps. He dropped a half-eaten peach, and looked round.

The gardener and Colonel Summers were running towards the hothouse, their faces livid with fury. Panic-stricken, William slipped, and the ladder went from under him, crashing through the glass.

Instinctively he grabbed at the nearest bough to save himself. There was a shower of peaches and the sound of wrenching as the supports gave way, and the whole tree came down.

The Colonel and his gardener gazed on the scene of destruction, paralysed with horror.

"I don't want to know what happened, William," said his aunt firmly an hour later. "Colonel Summers rang up to ask for your father's address, and I've given it to him. He sounded quite distraught. He's going to write to your father and make his complaint and demand damages. No, I don't want to hear anything more about it. Colonel Summers is going to write to your father."

William decided to go out for a long walk in the afternoon. Passing the gate of Uplands, he saw Mr Foulard smiling at him across the road. William stared at him.

"And how's my young friend?" Mr Foulard was saying.

William scowled, suspecting mockery or a trap, but Mr Foulard was taking some coins out of his pocket, was handing them to William, and saying heartily, "I suppose a little pocket-money never comes amiss? Unless boys have changed since my time, what?"

"Th-th-th-th-thanks," stammered William as he took the two half-crowns.

He couldn't think what had happened since yesterday.

What had happened since yesterday was that Mr Foulard had heard of the destruction of his rival's cherished peach tree, and was delighted by the now certain prospect of winning the first prize for both peaches and asparagus.

"Had tea?" went on Mr Foulard.

William shook his head.

"Come along, then," said Mr Foulard. "Come along!"

He led William up the short drive and in at the door of the house, beaming down at him.

This boy had done (in ten minutes) what he'd been trying in vain to do all these years: knocked out old Summers and his peaches.

"Now we'll see about a piece of plum cake, eh?" he said.

It was while William was just finishing a hearty tea that he got his next shock. Hearing voices outside, he looked up and saw a fat boy and his fat mother passing the window.

"Ah, my daughter and my little grandson,

Georgie," said Mr Foulard. "You haven't met them, have you?"

"Er – yes," said William. "Yes, I've met 'em, all right. I met 'em this afternoon."

"Splendid, splendid!" said Mr Foulard. "I'll go and tell them you're here."

William had indeed encountered the fat Georgie in the street an hour earlier, and had defended himself against Georgie's stone throwing.

William sat staring at the door, a half-eaten piece of plum cake in his hand. Scraps of conversation reached him.

"Not *that* boy!" came in the fat woman's voice. "Not that *dreadful* boy! The one that wrecked poor Colonel Summers' peaches?"

"Boys will be boys," came genially in Mr Foulard's voice. "Boys will be boys, you know. We mustn't be too hard on them."

"And he threw a stone at Georgie."

"Dear, dear!" said Mr Foulard. "That's bad, but – after all . . ." *After all*, he meant, *I shall owe my first prize to him.*

But Georgie's mother brushed him aside and entered the room, fixing a cold stare on William.

"Good afternoon," she said icily.

"Good afternoon," said William.

"You've finished your tea, haven't you?" said Georgie's mother. "I'm sure it's time you went home."

"All right," said William. "All right, I'm goin'—"

He scraped the crumbs on his plate carefully together, put them into his mouth, and withdrew.

Georgie unscrewed his face into a sly smile. He had thought of a plan. Chuckling to himself, he slipped out of the French windows.

William did not hurry. He might as well do a little exploring . . .

He wandered off the drive, took a look at the famous asparagus bed, then began to make his way slowly towards the front gate.

Suddenly a handful of mud struck him on the side of the face, filled his mouth and eyes, and ran down his collar. He had a vision of a fleeing figure and leapt to the pursuit.

Georgie fled as quickly as he could, hardly knowing where he was going, till he reached the asparagus bed. There, William caught him up, and dealt him a powerful blow on the nose that sent him sprawling among the cherished shoots.

Boys in this condition have little sense of property. The two did not even realise that they were fighting on a prize asparagus bed. They plunged and trampled and leapt and

wrestled. And by the end of five minutes the battleground was a muddy stew, garnished with a few asparagus stalks . . .

When William reached his aunt's house, it was to find that Mr Foulard had rung her up to demand his father's address. He was going to write at once to lodge his complaint and demand compensation for his asparagus bed.

William decided to go out for a walk once more . . .

He encountered Colonel Summers. Colonel Summers had only just received the news of the destruction of his rival's asparagus bed.

"I'm going away till tomorrow. Come in for that knife tomorrow morning. And about that letter . . ."

"Yes?" said William.

"Well, on the whole, I've decided not to send it . . . Boys will be boys . . . Come for your knife tomorrow."

And he went on down the road, leaving William staring after him in amazed relief.

He'd get the knife, after all – and there'd be

only one letter of complaint to his father instead of two.

And, he assured himself, he'd made things fair. They would get a prize each . . . If nothing else happened, of course . . .

But something else did happen.

William was wandering down the road that evening, his heart full of gratitude to Colonel Summers.

When, therefore, passing the Colonel's house, he saw a red glow through the trees, he thought it best to go and investigate.

Perhaps one of his outhouses was on fire. He could not omit this small service to his only friend.

He pushed the gate open and went to where he had seen the glow. It was all right. It was merely the remains of a garden fire.

Relieved, he went out and home again, leaving the gate open . . .

The news reached Mr Foulard just as he was writing the letter to William's father. Colonel

Summers' asparagus bed had been turned into a ploughed field overnight!

Someone had left the gate open, and twenty-five cattle had apparently danced the hornpipe on it! There was not a vestige of asparagus left!

A slow smile spread over his face. Poor old Summers. Peaches *and* asparagus gone. What a state he'd be in!

He saw in his mind's eye the published results of the show. "Mr H.B. Foulard – Hothouse Peaches – First Prize." And poor old Summers nowhere . . .

He began slowly to tear up his letter to William's father. Boys will be boys, he said to himself. No need to be too hard on the little blighter.

The next morning William made his way to Colonel Summers' house.

The Colonel received William coldly.

He did not know that William was responsible for the wreck of his asparagus

bed, but the wreck of it had brought back his earlier grievance about the peaches.

His mind's eye saw those same fatal words that Mr Foulard's saw: "Mr H.B. Foulard – Hothouse Peaches – First Prize."

"The knife?" he said. "What knife?"

"Th–the knife you promised me," stammered William.

"I think you must have misunderstood me. You can hardly expect me to give you one now."

"Well, I've done all I could to make up," pleaded William.

"What have you done?"

"Well, I came in 'cause I *thought* there was a fire, an' I wanted to put it out for you. I din't know it was only a garden fire when I came in."

Colonel Summers' face turned purple.

"So-it-was-*you*-who-left-the-gate-open?" he said between his teeth.

At that moment the door opened and a housemaid entered with a letter.

Colonel Summers took it, and read it.

It was from the Committee of the Flower Show, saying that, owing to war conditions, the show would not be held this year.

A slow smile spread over Colonel Summers' features. Saved! Saved at the eleventh hour! He wouldn't get any first prize, but neither would that worm Foulard.

"Well, well, well, well!" he said, smiling down at William. "What was it you came for? A knife, wasn't it?"

"Y-y-yes, yes, you said you'd—"

"Of course, of course," said the genial Colonel Summers. (Little devil, of course, but so were all boys. Boys will be boys. Poor old Foulard. Ha, ha! Poor old Foulard!)

"Now you can take your choice, my boy, I'll give you any one of them you like—"

It was the evening of William's return. He had gone upstairs to wash after the journey. Mr and Mrs Brown were sitting downstairs waiting for him.

"Odd those letters we had from Florence," said Mr Brown, "saying that William had done something dreadful, and that I should shortly be receiving appalling bills for damages from a Colonel Summers and a Mr Foulard."

At this point William entered. He looked shiningly clean and innocent.

"Well, did you have a nice time at your aunt's?" said Mrs Brown.

"Yes, thanks," said William.

"Anything – er – interesting happen?" said Mr Brown.

William considered.

"No. Nothin' really int'restin'."

"Let me see," said Mr Brown thoughtfully, "there was a Mr Foulard there, wasn't there? Did you have anything to do with him?"

William looked at his father impassively.

"Him?" he said, as if searching in the recesses of his memory. "Oh, yes. He gave me five shillin's an' invited me to tea."

"Oh, and what about – er – Colonel Summers?" said Mrs Brown.

William brought the Burmese knife out of his pocket.

"Yes, he was jolly nice, too. He gave me this."

Mr and Mrs Brown looked at each other and shrugged helplessly.

William the Great Actor

and Other Stories

Contents

William and the Princess Goldilocks

It was Robert, William's elder brother, who took him to the pantomime, not because he wanted to take him there, but because in a moment of weakness he had rashly promised to take him, and William had ruthlessly held him to the promise.

To William, the afternoon was one of unclouded bliss. He laughed at the comedians, he cheered the hero, he hissed the villain, and he fell in love with Princess Goldilocks, the heroine.

He could not help thinking that his passion was returned, for she seemed to smile directly

at him, to speak to him alone. As he followed the crowd out of the theatre, he felt that all the rest of his life must be devoted to her service.

During the next few days, William seemed to those around him to be strangely quiet. They could not, of course, know that in reality he was engaged on her behalf in desperate adventures – fighting armies of brigands single-handed, storming rocky strongholds, killing ferocious wild beasts. These adventures always terminated happily, and the rescued Princess Goldilocks flung herself into his arms sobbing out her gratitude and love.

Gradually, though, William began to find these adventures unconvincing. They left him exactly where he was before. He must betake himself to the sterner stuff of real life.

He decided to walk to London, make his way into her room at the theatre and ask her to marry him at once. He would take with him as much money as he could extract from his mother. Wearing an expression of almost painful virtue, he entered the drawing-room where his mother and his sister Ethel sat over the fire doing needlework.

"They say that an actress is staying at the Cedars," Ethel was saying as he entered.

"The Cedars?" said Mrs Brown vaguely.

"Yes . . . that place in Marleigh they've turned into a hotel, you know. They've been advertising it a lot – old-fashioned Christmas and that sort of thing. She goes up every day to London for the show."

"What show is she in?" asked Mrs Brown.

"A pantomime. The one that Robert took William to. She's Goldilocks or something. What's the matter, William? Do you want something?" But William had vanished. He was already on his way to Marleigh.

William knew the Cedars Hotel. He walked up its imposing drive, revolved its revolving doors, and found himself in a large hall. And here William realised suddenly that he did not even know his beloved's name. To demand to see Princess Goldilocks would merely draw down ridicule on himself. While he was cudgelling his brains for some plan of campaign, the gigantic hall porter approached him with evident disapproval.

"What do you want, my boy?" he demanded sternly.

An idea flashed into William's ready brain: "I've come to see someone what's staying here," he said.

"Who?" said the porter.

For a moment William was at a loss. He must ask for some imaginary person. Then,

while he waited, he could think out his plans.
But he couldn't think of a name . . . Suddenly
a word flashed into his mind – the name of the
only river in England that he had got right in
the last geography exam.

"Mr Medway," he said triumphantly.

The hall porter looked over his shoulder at
a lady behind a desk.

"Is Mr Medway in?" he said.

William's mouth dropped open in horror.

"I – I din' mean *that* Mr Medway," he said

hastily, but neither of them took any notice of him.

"Yes, he came in some time ago," said the lady behind the desk. She craned her neck to look down a corridor. "Here he is coming now."

Panic-stricken, William plunged back into the revolving doors. Hardly had he entered them, however, when he saw the familiar figure of Robert standing just outside the door, talking to a girl. He remembered that when Robert was in cash, he was fond of bringing his *inamorata* of the moment to tea at the Cedars Hotel. Hastily he pushed the doors inward to complete the circle.

By this time, however, a grim-looking man had entered the hotel hall, and the porter was talking to him, unmistakably pointing out William. With increasing panic, William pushed the door round again. Having done that, there seemed nothing for it but to go on pushing it round. One exit would bring him out to confront Robert, who by this time had seen him, the other would bring him out to confront Mr Medway.

William saw himself spending the rest of his life in the revolving doors, going round and round, till gradually he died of starvation. But someone of authority had arrived, and suddenly the door stopped. Robert, unwilling that his *inamorata* should learn his relationship to the young ruffian, had hastily remembered that the teas at the Cedars Hotel were very poor, and one could get a far better tea at the village inn. William, seeing the coast clear on that side, tried to escape to it, but the powerful hand of the porter held his ear, and dragged him back to the hotel foyer.

"Is this the boy who was asking for me?" said Mr Medway.

"Yes, sir," said the porter, giving William the look of one athirst for blood.

"I suppose you're my nephew Trevor," said Mr Medway sternly. "You arrive in a disgraceful state of untidiness, more than half an hour before the time at which I asked you to call for me, and then you make a fool of yourself and me over that door. A child in its cradle could have managed the thing better."

"I don't think it could," said William. "I mean, if it was in its cradle, it'd have to get out to push the door, and I don't think it could—"

"Be quiet," said Mr Medway testily. "And come into the lounge. If there's one thing I detest, it's being the centre of a scene."

"Well, you weren't," said William. "I don't see how you could have been, considering it was me that was in the door."

"Be *quiet*!" snapped Mr Medway again, leading the way into the lounge.

The porter was still directing his blood-thirsty look at William, and William could see, for the present, no alternative. He followed Mr Medway into the lounge.

Sitting down beside him on a deep settee, Mr Medway subjected him to a scrutiny that seemed to increase his disapproval.

"It never occurred to you, I suppose," he said coldly, "to brush your hair, or wash your face, or change your suit before you came to call for me?"

"No," said William quite simply, and without resentment.

"I've not seen you for ten years, and I certainly don't seem to have missed much. Well, how are things at home going on? How's your mother?"

"Very well, thank you," said William.

"Very well? She told me in her last letter that she was no better at all."

"Yes, that's what I meant. Didn't I say that? I meant to say that."

"You seem to me to be half-witted."

"Yes, I am," said William, thankfully accepting this explanation. "The doctor says I may get better some day, but at present I am a bit half-witted."

Mr Medway glanced at him suspiciously. "Don't try any of your funny tricks on me, my lad. Of course, I know all your family news by letter. How's Lucy?"

"She's very well, in a sort of way," said William guardedly. "I mean, in one sort of a way she's very well, and in another she isn't."

"Your mother said she was quite well when she last wrote."

"Oh, yes, she is. I meant she *is* quite well. She had a cold last week, that was all I meant. She – she—" William could never resist embroidering a story, and memories of a cold Ethel had caught the week before came to his aid. "She went to a dance and got hot dancing, and then went sitting out in the garden with the man she'd been dancing with without putting anything over her evening dress . . ."

Mr Medway was gazing at him in bewilderment. "But – but – Lucy's your mother's new dog, surely?" he said.

William blinked. "Oh, yes. Yes, of course. Yes . . . I didn't know you said Lucy. I thought you'd said some other name. I wasn't thinkin' what I was sayin' just for one minute."

"You seem to have a misplaced sense of humour."

"Yes," said William. "Yes, that's what I've got."

"Well, I must say I looked for a little more ordinary intelligence in a nephew of mine . . . Is Pongo all right?"

William's spirits rose. Pongo, of course, could be nothing but a dog. "Oh, yes. He's getting on fine."

"Feeding well?"

"Oh, yes. He has a dog biscuit every morning and some bones in the middle of the day."

"Dog biscuits! *Bones*!"

"Oh, he has more than that. He has all the scraps that are left on our plates."

"Dog biscuits . . . scraps on plates . . . is *that* any way to feed a two-year-old child?" thundered Mr Medway.

William realised that he had made another bad break. "That was just a joke. I mean, I was thinking of Lucy."

"Your mother said Lucy lived entirely on raw meat."

"Yes, she does," said the unhappy William. "I mean I was thinking of the dog next door."

Mr Medway rose abruptly. "I won't waste any more time on such rubbish. You'd better take me to your house now. Wait a minute, though. I really can't walk through the streets with you in such a state. You'd better come up to my bedroom and tidy yourself."

There seemed nothing for it but to comply.

Upstairs, in a palatial bedroom, Mr Medway turned on the washbasin taps. William, with an air of an intrepid hero facing unknown danger, plunged his face into the water, then began to scrub it vigorously. While he was engaged in this operation there came a knock at the door, and a boy entered. He was about William's age, but startlingly different in appearance – clean and neat, the shine of his hair rivalling the shine of his shoes.

"Who are you?" demanded Mr Medway.

"I'm Trevor, Uncle," said the apparition.

"Good Lord! Then who's this?"

William had raised his face from the washstand, and was watching them through a thick covering of soapsuds.

"That's William Brown, Uncle," said Trevor. "He's a very rough boy. Mother doesn't allow me to speak to him."

The face of Mr Medway became suffused with an angry purple. He started towards William. William dodged neatly and darted out of the room and along the passage. A large, open hamper near the lift seemed to offer a good hiding-place. He leapt into it, drawing down the lid, and waited. Soon he heard the voices of Trevor and Mr Medway.

"Which way did he go? The whole thing's outrageous. I'll speak to his father most strongly, and I hope he'll punish him."

"So do I, Uncle."

"Well," said Mr Medway, "we won't waste any more time on him. Come along." He opened the lift gate and their voices died away. William considered his position from the darkness of the hamper. It was not reassuring. He was marooned on the second floor of a large hotel, his escape cut off by a gigantic porter who was presumably thirsting for his blood. Suddenly he heard heavy footsteps approaching. He crouched in silence for some moments, then suddenly he felt himself swung unceremoniously into the air.

"It's 'eavy, mate," said a gruff voice. "Thought it was supposed to be empty."

William, holding his head in both hands to protect it, heard the sound of a door opening, and another voice saying, "'Ere's the 'amper,

Miss. An' proper 'eavy it is too."

"Nonsense," replied a sharp, feminine voice. "It can't be heavy. There is nothing in it. Put it down and go."

With a bang, the men flung down the hamper and departed.

"Cadging for a tip!" muttered the feminine voice indignantly. "Pretending it was heavy! What rubbish! Well, come on . . . we'd better get to work."

"Yes, Miss," said a second voice.

There was a quick movement, and the lid of the hamper was thrown back. William found himself gazing up into two faces. One was evidently that of a maid. The other was that of Princess Goldilocks.

But Princess Goldilocks did not look as she did on the stage. She looked older and less sweet. Much older and much less sweet. In fact, every trace of the radiant youth and sweetness that had so charmed William had vanished. At close quarters, she looked elderly – and irritable . . .

"What are you doing in that hamper?" said Princess Goldilocks, fixing an angry gaze upon him. William rose silently, returning her in imagination to the brigands and wild beasts from which he had in imagination so often rescued her.

"I said, what are you doing in that hamper?" snapped the lady again.

"I was mendin' it," said William distantly. "I was just passin', and I saw it wanted mendin', so I got in an' mended it, an' then those two men came an' carried it away, an' nearly broke my head off."

"I don't believe a word of it," said the lady furiously. "Show me *where* you've mended the hamper."

"Jus' there," said William, waving his hand in a gesture that included the entire room. "You naturally can't see where it's mended, because it's mended, an' it looks jus' like the rest of it. I'd jus' finished mendin' it when those men came along an' nearly broke my head off."

"I don't believe a *word* of it," said the lady again, stamping her foot. "You're a thief, that's what you are. Trying to gain entry to my rooms to steal my jewels. What's your name?"

"Trevor Monkton," said William promptly. "My uncle's staying in the hotel. He's called Mr Medway. He's a very rich man. Anyway, I can't stay any longer. I'm very busy this afternoon. Goodbye." He disappeared abruptly.

"Stop him," screamed Princess Goldilocks

to her maid. "Heaven *knows* what he's taken. Quick, quick, quick! Stop him!"

They both came running out after him towards the lift. William entered it calmly, closed the gates with slow deliberation, put his tongue out at them through the bars, then pressed the 'Ground Floor' button and vanished. Hysterical screams of "Stop thief!" followed him.

William emerged from the lift into the hall. The porter advanced to meet him with the air of one about to deal out a long-delayed vengeance. But when he came close to the lift, he stiffened and stood listening intently. Cries of "Stop thief!" still floated down the lift-well.

"Sounds like someone callin' for help," said William with an expression of innocent interest.

"Crikey!" said the big porter and, pushing William aside, he leapt into the lift, pressed a button and vanished from sight.

William was out of the unguarded door like

a flash of lightning. Like a flash of lightning, he shot along the road, and down the field path, till he reached the neighbourhood of his home. There he paused, drew breath, straightened his collar and tie, stroked back his spikes of hair, assumed his most effective swagger and, congratulating himself on having discovered the illusory nature of love before it was too late, sauntered slowly home to tea.

William the Great Actor

William was walking home. He was whistling. On the way, he met Douglas and Henry and Ginger.

"Hello," they said. "Where have you been?"

"I've been to a rehearsal," said William. "I'm actin' in a play."

They were impressed.

"What play?" demanded Ginger.

"Oh, one the Literary Society's gettin' up," said William, airily. "It's for raisin' money to get them a cinematograph, and me sixpence."

"What's the play called?" said Douglas.

William didn't know what it was called so he said, "Oh, that's a secret. I've not got to tell anyone that."

"Oh, what are you actin' in it?" said Henry.

"I – I'm the most important person in it," said William. "They jolly well couldn't do it at all without me."

"You the hero?" said Ginger incredulously.

"Ah yes," admitted William. "That's what I am."

In fact, the secretary of the Literary Society, Mrs Monkton-Bruce, desperate for someone to reproduce the sound effects, had commandeered William's services. William, equally desperate to purchase a new football, had accepted their miserly offer of sixpence to be the whistling wind and other assorted offstage noises. "They're all women," William continued, "so, of course, they had to get a man in from somewhere to be the hero."

The Outlaws were not quite convinced.

"Well," said Ginger, "I s'pose if you're the hero, you'll be havin' rehearsals with them?"

"Yes, course I will."

"All right," challenged Ginger. "Tell us when you're havin' the next one and we'll see."

So, next Tuesday at three o'clock, hidden in the bushes in Mrs Monkton-Bruce's garden, they saw the cast of *The Trial of Love* arrive one by one at the front door and with them arrived William, the only male character, swaggering self-consciously up Mrs Monkton-Bruce's front drive.

The Outlaws were deeply impressed. It was true; William *must* be the hero of the play.

He wasn't summoned to another rehearsal for a fortnight. The play was, as Miss Georgina Hemminsley said, "Taking shape beautifully". Miss Hemminsley, as a Cavalier, looked quite dashing despite her 40-odd years and Miss Featherstone, as the Roundhead, looked also very fine though she too had passed her first youth. Miss Gladwin, they all agreed, made a sweetly pretty heroine.

William arrived with his paraphernalia of

coconuts and squibs and tin tray and, he considered, put up the best show of all of them. True the rest of the cast seemed a little irritable. They kept saying, "Quietly, William! William, not so *loud.*"

At the end, Miss Green-Jones, who seemed strangely excited, burst out, "Now I've got some news for you all. You'll never *guess* who's staying in the village."

"Who?" chorused the cast breathlessly.

"Sir Giles Hampton, the actor!"

The cast uttered screams of excitement.

"He's had a nervous breakdown," said Miss Green-Jones, "and he's staying in the inn here because of the air and he's supposed to be incognito but *of course*, people recognised him. As a matter of fact, he's telling people who he is because he's not really keen on being incognito. Actors never are really. They feel frightfully mad if people don't recognise them."

"Do you think he'll come?" said all the cast simultaneously.

"I – I don't know but – oh, William, you needn't stay. Go home."

William was annoyed at this unceremonious ejection. He walked down the road scowling morosely, and collided with a tall man with bushy eyebrows.

"You should look where you're going, old son," said the stranger.

"Come to that, so should you," remarked William.

The tall man blinked. "Do you know who I am?"

"No," said William, "and I bet you don't know who I am either."

"I am a very great actor," said the man.

"So am I," said William promptly.

"So great," went on the man, "that when they want me to play a part, they give me any money I choose to ask for it."

"I'm that sort too. I asked for sixpence an' they give it me straight off. It's going towards a new football."

"And you know why I'm here, old son?" said the stranger.

"No," said William, and added, "I'm here because I live here."

"Oh. I'm here because of my nerves. Acting has exhausted my vitality and impaired my nervous system. I am highly strung. Do you know that sometimes before I go on the stage I tremble from head to foot?"

"I don't. I never feel like that when I'm actin'."

"Ah ha," smiled the stranger. "But I'm always the most important person in the plays I act in."

"So am I. I'm like that. I'm the most important person in the play I'm in now."

"Would you like to see the programme of the play I've just been acting in, in London?" continued the actor, taking a piece of paper out of his pocket.

William looked at it. It contained a list of names in ordinary sized print then an "and" and then – GILES HAMPTON in large letters. "Oh yes," said William calmly. "That's the way my name's going to be printed at our play."

"What play is it?" said the man yielding at last to William's irresistible egotism.

"It's called *The Trial of Love*. It's for my football and their cinematograph."

"Ah ha, and may, um, distinguished strangers come to it?"

"Oh yes, anyone can come to it. You've got to pay, everyone's got to pay."

"Well, old son," said the distinguished stranger, "I must certainly come and see you play the hero."

The dress rehearsal was not an unqualified success.

"Thunder, William!" said Miss Gladwin irritably. "Why don't you keep awake and follow where we are?"

William beat on his tin tray. Miss Green-Jones groaned. "Oh that noise," she said.

"Goes through and through my head. I can't bear it!"

"Well, thunder *is* loud," said William coldly. "It's naturally loud, I can't help thunder bein' naturally loud." Gloomily he returned to his meditations. He'd seen the programme and his name wasn't on it at all. If it hadn't been for that sixpence, he'd certainly have chucked the whole thing.

They had got to the snowstorm scene now. The curtains were half drawn across and in the narrow aperture appeared Miss Gladwin, the heroine. She said, "How cold it is. Heaven, wilt thou show me no pity?" and turned up her face to the sky and tiny snowflakes began to fall upon her face. The tiny "snowflakes" were bits of paper dropped down through an opening in the ceiling by her well-mannered little nephew.

It was the evening of the performance. There were frenzied preparations behind the scenes.

William was to hand out the programmes.

He stood sphinx-like at the door of the village hall, distributing them. He devised a means by which he hoped to vindicate his position as hero. He had laboriously printed out four special programmes. He had copied down the *dramatis personae* from the ordinary programme. But at the end he had put an "and" and then in gigantic letters – WIND, RAIN, HORSES' HOOVES, SHOTS AND ALL OTHER NOISES – WILLIAM BROWN. Seeing the Outlaws coming he hastily got three of his home-made programmes out and handed them over.

"Good ole William," murmured Ginger.

"Why aren't you changin' into your things?" said Henry.

"Well, I – I – I don't actually come on to the stage," admitted William. "I'm the most important person in the play as you'll soon jolly well see but I don't *actually* come on to the stage."

He was glad to have got that confession off his chest. There was only one special programme left. That was for the actor – *if* the actor came . . . and, yes, there he was. He carried a parcel under his arm. The actor entered the hall. William thrust the programme into his hand.

"Hmm, thought you were the hero," said the actor gazing at him sardonically.

William met his gaze unblinkingly. "I am, but the hero doesn't always come on to the stage. Not in the newest sort of plays anyway." He pointed to the programme. "That's me," he said modestly. "All of it's me." With this, he hastened back behind the curtain.

The play began. There was his cue. Someone was saying, "How the storm rages – canst hear the wind?"

At the ensuing sound the prompter dropped her book and the heroine lost her balance and brought down the mantelpiece on top of her. William had put his fingers into each corner of his mouth in order to aid nature in the rendering of the storm. The sound was more piercing than even he had expected it to be.

"That," thought William complacently, noticing the havoc it played with both audience and cast, "was something like a wind." That'll show them whether he was the hero of the play or not.

The cast pulled itself together and continued.

William's next cue was the thunder.

"Listen," said the heroine. "Listen how the thunder rages in the valley."

The thunder raged, and continued to rage. For some minutes the cast remained silent and motionless, waiting for the thunder to abate, but as it showed no signs of stopping they tried to proceed. It was, however, raging so violently that no one could hear a word so they had to stop again. At last, even its maker tired of it and it died away. The play proceeded.

William's next cue was the horses' hooves and he was feeling a little nervous about that. The sound of horses' hooves was made with a coconut and though William managed to take his coconut about with him all the time the play was in rehearsal, he had last night succumbed to temptation, broken it up and eaten it.

"Listen," Miss Gladwin was saying. "Listen, I hear the sound of horses' hooves." Then in the silence came the sound of a tin tray being hit slowly, loudly and regularly.

The audience gave a yell of laughter. William felt annoyed. It wasn't anything to laugh at. He showed his annoyance with another deafening thunderstorm. When this had died away the play proceeded. But

William didn't wish to withdraw from the public eye. It had occurred to him that the civil war must be going on all the time. He had better throw a few squibs about and make a bit more wind and thunder. He set to work with commendable thoroughness.

At long last the end of the scene came. Mr Flurster drew the curtains, and chaos reigned. Most of the cast attacked William but some of them were attacking each other and quite a lot of them were attacking the prompter. Fortunately for William, however, there was little time for recrimination as the audience was already clamouring for the second scene. This was the snowstorm scene. Miss Gladwin had installed her beautifully mannered nephew in the loft earlier in the evening with a box of chocolate creams to keep him quiet.

Miss Gladwin went on to the stage and leapt into her monologue. William, behind the scenes, relapsed into boredom. He was roused from it by Miss Gladwin's nephew, who came down the steps of the loft, carrying an empty chocolate box and looking green. "William," he said, "will you do my thing for me – I'm going to be sick."

"All right," said William. "What do you do?"

"You just get the bucket in the corridor and take it up to the loft and empty it over her slowly when she turns up her face."

It was not William's fault that someone had put the stage fireplace in the passage and in such a position that it completely hid the bucket of torn-up paper. The only bucket visible was the bucket of water placed there in case of fire. William took it up and went to the stairs leading into the loft.

"Oh, it's jolly heavy – water, crumbs!" He hadn't realised that it was water. He had an idea that it was torn-up paper for snow but probably they had changed their minds and thought they'd have rain instead. He took it very carefully up the stairs, then knelt over the little opening where he could see Miss

Gladwin down below. He was only just in time.

She was already saying, "How cold it is! Heaven, wilt thou show me no pity?" Then, with a beautiful gesture of despair, she raised her face towards the ceiling to receive full and square the entire contents of a bucket of water.

William tried to do it slowly but it was a heavy bucket and he had to empty it all at

once. He considered it rather clever that he was hitting her face so exactly.

For a moment the audience enjoyed the spectacle of Miss Gladwin sitting on the floor, dripping wet and gasping and spluttering. And then Mr Flurster had the presence of mind to draw the curtain. Then the entire cast began to look for William. They knew by instinct who was responsible for the calamity.

William, realising also by instinct that he had made a mistake, slipped out into the darkness. He was stopped by a magisterial figure that blocked his way.

"Ah ha, going already, old son? I had meant to present this to you at the end, but pray accept it now."

He went away chuckling and William found himself clasping the most magnificent football he had ever seen in his life. And that was not all, for the next day there arrived a magnificent cinematograph for the Literary Society, sent by Sir Giles Hampton, with a note telling them that their little play had completely cured his nervous breakdown and that it would be a precious memory to him all the rest of his life and he was going back to London cheered and invigorated.

And that was not all. There arrived for William some weeks later two tickets for a box at a London theatre. William went, accompanied by his mother. He came back and told the Outlaws all about it. He said he had seen a play called *Macbeth* and though he thought it quite funny, he could have made a much better storm himself.

A Bit of Blackmail

Bob Andrews was one of the picturesque figures of the village. He lived in the East Lodge of The Hall and was supposed to help with the gardening of The Hall grounds. He was tall, white-bearded and gloriously lazy. He had a roguish twinkle in his blue eyes and a genius for wasting time, both his own and other people's. He was a great friend of William and the Outlaws. He seemed to them to be free from all the drawbacks that usually accompanied the state of grown-upness. He was never busy, never disapproving, *never* tidy. He could carve boats out of wood and make whistles and bows and arrows and tops. He was paid a regular salary by the owner of The Hall for occasionally opening the lodge gates and, still more occasionally, assisting with the gardening.

Mr Bott, the new owner of The Hall, was a businessman. Mr Bott of Bott's Sauce believed in getting the last ounce of work out of his work-people. That was what had raised Mr Bott from grocer's errand boy to Lord of the Manor. When Mr Bott discovered that he had upon his newly acquired estate a man who drew a working man's salary for merely standing about, he promptly sacked that man. It would have been against Mr Bott's most sacred principles to do otherwise.

The Outlaws had avoided Mr Bott's estate because of his daughter, Violet Elizabeth. But having heard that she had departed on a lengthy visit to distant relatives, the Outlaws decided to return to their favourite haunts.

"Let's go an' find Bob," said William.

They made their way to the East Lodge.

Bob stood at his door. "Hello, Bob," called the Outlaws.

"Halloo, yer youn' rascals!"

"I say, Bob, make us some boats an' then let's have a race."

"Sure an' I will!" said Bob, knocking out his pipe and taking a large penknife out of his pocket. "Tho it's wastin' m' time y'are, as usual."

He took out a piece of wood and began to whittle.

"How's the squirrel, Bob?"

"Oh, fine."

"Bob, they're building in the ivy on the old oak again."

"Sure an' I knew that before you did, me boy."

But though he whittled and whistled, Bob was evidently *not* his old self.

"I say, Bob, next month—"

"Next month, me boys – I shall not be here."

They stared at him open-mouthed.

"What! You're goin' away for a holiday, Bob?"

"I'm goin' away, me boys, because the ol' devil up there has given me the sack. God forgive 'im, fer I won't!" he ended piously.

"But – *why*?" they said, aghast.

"He says I don't work. Me! And me wearin' me hands to the bone fer 'im the way I do."

"Huh! What a shame!" said the Outlaws.

"Turnin' me out into the col' world – may God forgive 'im! Well, here's yer boats, yer young rascals, an' don't go near me pheasant's nest or I'll put the fear of God 'n ye!"

"We've gotta *do* somethin'," said William, when Bob had returned, smoking peacefully, to his lodge.

"We can't do anythin'," said Ginger despondently. "Who'd take any notice of us anyway?"

William, the leader, looked at him sternly. "You just wait an' see," he said.

Mr Bott was very stout. His stoutness was a great secret trouble to Mr Bott. Mr Bott had made his money and now Mr Bott wished to take his proper place in society. Mr Bott considered, not unreasonably, that his corpulence detracted from his refinement of appearance. Mrs Bott frequently urged him to *do* something about it. He'd consulted many expensive specialists. Mrs Bott kept finding new men for him. The last new man she'd found practically guaranteed his treatment would transform a human balloon to a human pencil in a few months.

Every morning as soon as it was light, Mr Bott, decently covered by a large overcoat, went down to a small lake in the grounds among the bushes. There, Mr Bott divested himself of his overcoat and appeared in small bathing drawers. From the pockets of his overcoat, Mr Bott would then take a skipping rope and with this would skip five times round the lake. Then he would do his exercises. He would twist his short, fat body into strange attitudes, standing upon one short, fat leg, with the other thrust out at various angles and, invariably, overbalancing. Finally, Mr Bott had to plunge into the lake – it was not deep – splash and kick and run around in it and then emerge to dry himself with a towel, concealed in the other pocket of his overcoat, shiveringly don the overcoat again and, furtively, return to the house. For Mr Bott was shy about his early morning adventures.

One chilly morning, Mr Bott had skipped and leapt and twisted and splashed and

emerged, shivering and red-nosed, in readiness for his overcoat. But Mr Bott received a shock. His overcoat was not there. He looked all round the tree where he knew he'd left it and it was *not* there, it was most certainly not there. Mr Bott threw a glance of pathetic despair around him. Then, above the sound of his chattering teeth, he heard a voice.

"I've got your coat up here."

Mr Bott threw a startled glance up into the tree. For, among the leaves, a stern, freckled, wild-haired face glared down at him.

"I'll give you your coat," said William, "for your promise to let Bob stay."

Mr Bott clasped his dripping head with a dripping hand. "Bob?"

"Bob Andrews what you're sendin' away for nothin'."

Mr Bott tried to look dignified in spite of the chattering of his teeth and the water that poured from his hair down his face. "I have my reasons, my child," he said, "of which you know nothin'. Will you kindly give me back my coat? I'm afraid you're a very naughty, ill-behaved little boy to do a thing like this and if you aren't careful I shall tell the police about it."

"I'll give you your coat if you promise not to send Bob away," said William again, sternly.

"I shall most certainly speak to your father *and* the police," said Mr Bott. "You're a very impertinent little boy. Give me my coat at once!"

"I'll give you your coat," said William again, "if you'll promise not to send Bob away."

Mr Bott's dignity began to melt away. "Y – y – you young devil." He looked wildly around. In the long grass behind the tree lay a ladder that had been left there long ago by some gardener. With a yell of triumph, Mr Bott rushed to it.

"Oh crumbs," said William, among the leafage.

Mr Bott put the ladder against the tree trunk and began to swarm up it, large, dripping, chattering with rage and cold. William retreated along his branch, still clinging to the overcoat. Mr Bott pursued him furiously. "You young rogue, you young devil, I'll teach you, I'll—"

The branch down which William was retreating was directly over the lake. William alone it could easily have supported but it drew the line at Mr Bott. With a creaking and a crashing above which rose a yell of terror

214

from Mr Bott, it fell into the water, accompanied by its two occupants. The splash made by Mr Bott's falling body at first obscured the landscape.

Before William could recover, Mr Bott was upon him, maddened by rage and fury and wet and cold. He ducked William and shook William and tore his wet overcoat from William. William butted Mr Bott in his largest and roundest part, then scrambled from the lake and fled dripping towards the gate. Mr Bott at first pursued him then, realising that the path was taking him within sight of the high road, turned back, drew his soaked overcoat over his shoulders and fled, chatteringly and shiveringly, towards his splendid mansion.

Two hours later, William met the other Outlaws in the old barn where all their meetings were held.

"Well?" said the Outlaws eagerly.

William, who was wearing his best suit, looked pale but nonetheless determined. "Ah, hmm, it didn't quite come off," he admitted. "Somethin' went wrong. But I've jolly well not finished yet."

They looked at him with awe and respect.

"We'll have another meeting 'n three days," said William, "an – an – an' well, you just wait an' see."

The next day was bright and sunny. Mr Bott almost enjoyed his early morning exercises. He thought occasionally, with indignation, of the events of the previous morning. "That dreadful boy. Anyway, I've shown 'im. He isn't likely to come again after yesterday and, most certainly, Bob Andrews should go." Huh! He'd like any fool boy dictating to *him*.

But Mr Bott could not feel bad-tempered for long. It was such a bright sunny morning and he'd just discovered himself to be a seventh to an eighth of an inch thinner round the waist than this time last week. He leapt and skipped and gambled and splashed.

Once he imagined he saw the horrible boy's face in the bushes, but looking again he came to the conclusion that he must have been mistaken. Once, too, he thought he heard a snap or a crack as if someone had stepped on a twig, but listening again he came to the conclusion that he must have been mistaken.

He enjoyed his exercises for the next two mornings as well. But on the third morning, as soon as he'd come downstairs dressed and glowing to go to his study after his exercises, to look at his letters before breakfast, the butler threw open the door and announced, "They said it was important business, sir, and you knew about it. I hope it's all right."

Then four boys walked up to his desk. One was the boy who'd taken his overcoat up a tree two days before. The butler had gone.

Mr Bott, sputtering with rage, reached out to the bell. He was going to say, "Kick these boys out", when the worst of the boys, "the devil", laid half a dozen snapshots on his desk. Mr Bott looked at them – and then sat rigid and motionless, his hand still outstretched towards the bell. His ruby face grew pale.

The first snapshot showed Mr Bott, short, fat and, except for his microscopic bathing drawers, naked, skipping by the lake. The angle of his legs was irresistibly comic. The second snapshot showed Mr Bott, still short and fat and almost naked, balancing himself on one arm and one leg. The others stuck out wildly in the air, his eyes staring, his tongue hanging out of his mouth. The third snapshot showed Mr Bott in the act of overbalancing in a rather difficult exercise – that was the gem of the collection. The fourth showed Mr Bott lying on his back and kicking his legs in the air. The fifth showed Mr Bott standing on two very stiff arms and stiff legs with an expression of acute suffering on his face. The sixth showed Mr Bott splashing in the lake.

Mr Bott took out his handkerchief and wiped away the perspiration that was standing out on his brow.

"If you burn 'em," said William firmly, "we can get more. We've got the films an' we can make hundreds more an' jolly good ones too."

Mr Bott began to stammer. "I'm – I'm, er, wh – wh – what are you goin' t' do with them?" he asked.

"Just show 'em to people," said William calmly.

Horrid visions passed before Mr Bott's eye. He saw the wretched things in the local paper. He saw them pass from hand to hand in drawing-rooms. He saw strong men helpless with mirth as they seized on them. His position in society! Well, the less said about his position in society if those things became public, the better.

William took a crumpled document from his pocket and laid it solemnly upon Mr Bott's desk. "That's a contrack," he said, "signed in all our life's blood sayin' we'll keep 'em hid safely and never show 'em to anyone s' long as you let Bob stay."

Mr Bott knew when he was beaten. He moistened his lips. "All right, all right, I promise, only – only, go away." They went away.

Mrs Bott came in. Mr Bott still sat, huddled in his chair. "Oh, you don't look well, Botty, darling," said Mrs Bott.

"No," said Mr Bott in a hollow voice. "I don't know that this treatment's doin' me any good."

"Oh, isn't it, ducky? Well, I'll try to find you a new man."

*

That afternoon, the Outlaws passed Bob. He
stood outside his lodge, hands in pockets, pipe
in mouth, white-bearded, gloriously lazy.
"I've found a grass snake for yer, me boys," he
sang out. "He's in a box in the yard, beyon'.
Oh, an' Bob Andrews is not goin', me boys.
The sack is withdrawn. The ol' devil's realised
me value. Glory be to God!"

*

That night, Robert, William's elder brother, came downstairs with his camera in his hand. "I say," he said, "I could've sworn I put this away with half a dozen exposures left."

"Oh, when did you last have it, dear?" said his mother.

William took a book from a shelf and sat down at the table, resting his head on his hands.

"I put it away last autumn until the decent weather came round, but I could've sworn I put it away with a roll of film in." Robert's eye fell sternly and accusingly upon William.

William looked up and met it unflinchingly with an expression of patient endurance on his face. "Robert," he said with a sigh, "I wish you'd talk more quietly. I'm trying to learn my history dates."

Robert's jaw dropped. Then he went quietly from the room still gaping. There was simply no making head or tail of that kid.

William and the Fairy Daffodil

William had been on one of his long expeditions in Croome Woods. In his imagination he was an intrepid explorer searching for a lost tribe, cutting his way through dense jungle where no man had ever set foot before. The virgin forest had certainly left its mark upon him. It had clutched at his collar and hair with its thorn bushes. It had besmeared his face and clothes and knees and boots impartially with bogs . . .

Suddenly he found himself at the edge of the wood. There ahead of him was a large garden – and a large house. It didn't look like an ordinary house. Its windows were uncurtained. Within sat many girls of all sizes, with bobbed hair or plaits. Surprised and interested, he crept nearer.

A small woman wearing glasses stepped out of a French window and called to him. "Here, boy!" she said imperiously. William was uncertain whether to obey or to flee. But a small girl with a dimpled face and dark curly hair looked out of the window and smiled at him, and William obeyed.

He entered a classroom with a dais at one end. A large number of girls sat about the room at easels. The lady with spectacles took William by his ear, and led him up the room.

"The little model I had arranged for is unable to come, girls," she said, "so I am going to ask you to draw the gardener's boy."

"It must be a new gardener's boy," said a tall thin girl. "I've not seen him before."

"Don't talk, Gladys," said the mistress. "The point is not whether he is a new or old gardener's boy. The point is that you are to

224

draw him. Sit down, boy."

William, who had already picked out the dimpled, dark-haired little girl by the window, sat down quite meekly.

A girl in the front row gave a shudder. "Isn't he *dirty*?" she said.

"Never mind," said the mistress. "I want to draw him as he is – just an ugly, dirty little boy."

She apparently looked upon William as something as inanimate as a plaster-cast, but the ferocious glare which he now turned on her informed her that he was not.

"Er – try to look a little more pleasant, boy," she said faintly.

"I do hate having to draw *ugly* things," said the girl in the front row, with another shudder.

A look of apoplectic fury overspread William's face. But the little girl at the window with dimples and dark curls said, "*I* don't think he's ugly."

William's expression of fury turned into a sheepish smirk.

"Don't talk about him, children," said the lady. "*Draw* him."

They worked in silence. William looked about him. The frowning, critical, appraising glare of sixteen girls did not embarrass him at all. Only when he caught the eye of the little girl with the dimples did a dark blush over-spread his earth-bedecked countenance.

"I think I've got his *ugliness* all right," said a short, snub-nosed girl earnestly. "But I can't quite get his *cross* look."

"Let me see, dear," said the mistress. She took the sketch, and examined it. William craned his neck and looked with interest at his portrait. Certainly the sketch suggested a gorilla rather than a human being.

"Y-yes," said the mistress doubtfully, "you've caught a certain likeness—"

William opened his mouth indignantly, when the girl by the window said suddenly, "*I* don't think he looks cross."

William closed his mouth and his ferocity

softened once more into a sheepish grin.

"He keeps looking *diff'rent*," complained a girl in the back row.

"Stay the same, boy," ordered the mistress imperiously.

At that minute, a bell rang and there was a stampede of girls out of the doorway.

"Gently, girls," said the mistress, preparing to follow them. "Boy, stay and straighten up the room, and put the easels away."

William stayed behind and, to his joy, discovered that the little girl was staying behind too. She remained at her easel, gazing out of the window. William began to move easels about, without any definite plan of campaign. "I'm not the gardener's boy," he said to the little girl.

She did not answer.

"I'm an explorer."

She made no comment.

"I've explored places where no man ever set his feet before."

Still no answer.

"I once had all my teeth out without gas," he went on with deliberate untruthfulness, but with a vague desire to restore his self-respect.

Suddenly the little girl put down her head on her arms, and began to cry.

"Oh, don't," said William, greatly distressed. "What's the matter? Have you got toothache?"

"No-o!"

"Has anyone been unkind to you?"

"No-o-o-o! I'm homesick," wailed the little girl. "I want to go ho-o-o-ome."

"Well – well, you *go* home, then," counselled William, encouragingly. "You *go* home. I'll – I'll *take* you home."

"I c-c-can't."

"Why not?"

She dried her eyes. "Well, I'm in a play we're doing this afternoon, and if I don't turn up for it, they'll know something's happened and they'll c-c-catch me before I get to the station and bring me b-b-back!"

"No, they *won't*," said William. "I'll help you. I tell you, no one'll ever dare stop me. I've been where no man ever set his feet 'n I've—"

"Yes," said the little girl, quite unimpressed. "But don't you see? I can't go at once 'cause I've not had dinner yet, an' I'm hungry, an' if I run away after dinner, they'll find out at once and c-c-catch me."

She burst into sobs again.

"No, don't," said William desperately,

230

"don't cry. It's all right. I'll take care of you. I-I say," – the light of inspiration shone suddenly in his face – "I'll take your part in the play an' then they'll never know you've gone, an' you'll get home all right."

She stopped crying and gazed at him, then the hope died from her face and she burst into a wail. "B-b-but you don't look like a fa-a-a-airy," she sobbed.

"I could *make* myself look like one," said William grimly. "I bet I could! Look – look at me now."

He gazed into the distance, his features composed into a simper that suggested to an impartial observer a mixture of coyness and imbecility.

"Oh, no-o-o-o!" she wailed. "It doesn't – Oh, *don't*!"

"Well," he said, "if it looks wrong, can't I cover my face or somethin'?"

Her tears ceased. Her eyes shone. "Oh, I *forgot*!" she said. "There's a veil. They won't see your face. Oh you are a *nice* boy. Will you *really* do it? Listen, I'll tell you *just* what to do. I'm Fairy Daffodil – I'll get the clothes in a second. There's a cap of daffodil petals and a veil that comes down from them over your face, so *that's* all right. And you have to hide behind the green bank, at the side of the stage behind a lot of green stuff and leaves. You go there early, about two, and then when the others come they'll be so busy getting ready that they won't bother you. And when it begins you wait there till someone calls, 'Fairy Daffodil', and then you come out and bow and say, 'Here am I – speak, Queen.' And when that bit's over, you just sit down on the stool by the side of the queen's throne and you don't speak again. It's quite easy. Oh, it is *kind* of you, dear boy . . ."

William's freckled countenance flamed again. "Oh, it's nothing," he said modestly. "Why, I've been where no man's ever set his feet before. This is *nothing* to that."

The guests swarmed into the school hall. In

232

the middle of the second row sat William's father and mother, Mr and Mrs Brown. The room was tastefully decorated with leaves and bracken.

"I like to come to all these things, don't you?" said the man next to Mrs Brown. "And they're always very good about sending out invitations to all their little affairs."

"Oh, yes," said Mrs Brown vaguely, "and it looks very nice."

The curtain rose and the two grown ups continued their conversation in a whisper. "Well, I must say," said Mrs Brown, "I like to get right away from home sometimes, because, really, at home I'm on pins the whole time, not knowing what William's going to do next. At a place like this I feel *safe*. It's nice to be anywhere where I *know* William can't rise up before my eyes doing something awful."

"Fairy Daffodil!" called the fairy herald on the stage.

A figure arose from behind a leafy barrier, took an ungraceful step forward, tripped over the leafy barrier and crashed to earth, leafy barrier and all. The yellow head gear rolled off on to the floor revealing a tousled head, over a stern, earth-streaked face.

"What's your boy like?" said Mrs Brown's neighbour, who was not looking at the stage. "I don't think I've ever seen him."

But Mrs Brown's smile had faded. Her face had become a mask of horror. Her neighbour followed her eyes to the stage. The strange apparition was in no way disconcerted by the

contretemps with the leafy barrier. It did not even trouble to recover its head gear. It stood in the middle of the stage and said, loudly and ferociously, "Here I am."

There was dead silence. Fairy Bluebell, who stood near, inspired by a gallant determination to carry on in spite of all disasters, prompted, "Speak—"

William looked at her haughtily. "I've just spoke," he said.

"Speak, Queen," hissed Bluebell desperately.

"It's not my turn," hissed the queen back.

Bluebell stamped, "Say, 'Speak, Queen',", she said to William.

"Oh," said William. "I'm sorry, I forgot that bit. I forgot there was something else. Speak, Queen. That's all, anyway, isn't it? Where's the stool?" He looked round, then calmly sat down on the stool, sublimely unaware of actors and audience completely paralysed around him.

Slowly, very slowly, the power of speech returned to Mrs Brown. Her horror-stricken eyes left the stage. She clasped her husband's arm. "John," she said hysterically. "It-it-it's William."

Mr Brown, too, had gazed open-mouthed at this wholly unexpected apparition of his son. Then he recovered himself. "Er – nonsense, my dear," he said firmly. "Never seen the boy before. Do you hear? We've never seen the boy before."

"B-b-b-but we have, John," she said. "It's William!"

"Who's William?" said Mr Brown, wildly. "There isn't any William. Temporarily, I've disowned him. I've disowned him till we meet again under the shelter of our own roof. I don't know how he got here, or what he's going to do, and I don't care. He's nothing to do with me. I've disowned him, I tell you."

"Oh, John," wailed Mrs Brown. "Isn't it *awful*!"

Everyone agreed afterwards that somebody ought to have done something at once. But the headmistress was out of the room supervising the tea arrangements and the mistress who was prompting said that for all she knew it was some fresh arrangement made behind her back. Anyway, the play dragged on. But no one took any further interest in the play. The whole interest of the audience was concentrated on the curious apparition, inadequately clothed in yellow butter-muslin, who had taken its seat at the foot of the throne.

The apparition itself seemed unaware that

it was attracting any attention. It sat down and gazed around it, stern, bored, contemptuous – then alight as some happy memory came into its face. It pulled up the butter-muslin to its waist, revealing muddy boots, muddy legs and muddy trousers, plunged its hand into its pocket and brought out a nut, which it proceeded to crack with much facial contortion and bared teeth.

At this point the headmistress entered by the door at the back of the hall. Her face wore a proud smile. Her eyes wandered slowly to the stage. The proud smile dropped from her face. The Fairy Daffodil had cracked the nut and was proceeding with every appearance of concentration and satisfaction to extract the edible part of it.

With the air of one dashing to a heroic rescue, the headmistress plunged up the hall, drew the curtain and made a grab at the Fairy Daffodil. "What is the meaning of this, you wicked boy!" she said.

The Fairy Daffodil abandoned his half-eaten nut, dodged what he rightly suspected to be an avenging hand, and fled.

"Catch him," panted the headmistress. "Catch that boy!"

The entire cast followed by the entire staff dashed after William. Gathering up his impeding yellow robe, William fled like an arrow from a bow out of a door at the back of the hall, across the garden towards the front gate. He would probably have outrun his pursuers, had he not collided with a little girl and a tall man who were just entering.

The little girl gave a cry of joy and said, "Oh, it's the nice boy, Daddy." Then to William, "I met Daddy on the way to the station, boy. I didn't know he was coming and I feel quite happy now. He's given me a lovely tip, and I've remembered that I'm playing in the netball match next week, and I'd *hate* to miss that."

At this point the gym mistress, the vanguard of the pursuit, arrived and seized William by one ear; the art mistress arrived

next and seized him by the other ear. The head
girl arrived next and, not wanting to be out of
it, seized him by the scruff of his neck. Thus
seized at all available points, he was marched
off to the headmistress.

It was an hour later. The visitors had been
collected again. The prizes had been distri-
buted. The headmistress, at the earnest request
of the tall man, had pardoned William's
escapade. The visitors were having tea in the

garden. William sat at a little table with the tall man and the little girl. He was blissfully happy. He was consuming unlimited quantities of cakes, and every now and then the little girl smiled at him, very sweetly.

"I won't be so silly any more, Daddy," she said.

"One minute," said her father. "I can see a business friend of mine there. Hello, Brown," he called.

"This is my daughter, Brown," said the tall man.

William tried to avoid his father's gaze.

"I'm not sure who this youngster is, so I can't introduce him properly. All I know about him is that he's been where no man ever set foot before and he's had all his teeth taken out without gas – but perhaps you know him?"

"I didn't know either of those facts about him," admitted Mr Brown drily, "but," – his sardonic eye forced his son's to meet it – "I *have* met him before."

Meet Just William

Whether he's getting into adventures with his band
of Outlaws or driving his family crazy, there's
never a dull moment with William Brown around!

A bumper collection of funny stories about Just
William, specially adapted for younger readers
by Martin Jarvis – the famous 'voice of William'
on radio and bestselling audio.

Contains the first three MEET JUST WILLIAM books:

WILLIAM'S BIRTHDAY AND OTHER STORIES

**WILLIAM AND THE HIDDEN TREASURE AND
OTHER STORIES**

WILLIAM'S WONDERFUL PLAN AND OTHER STORIES.

A selected list of titles available from Macmillan Children's Books

The prices shown below are correct at the time of going to press. However, Macmillan Publishers reserves the right to show new retail prices on covers, which may differ from those previously advertised.

Richmal Compton

| Meet Just William | 978-0-330-45343-1 | £5.99 |

Miles Gibson and Neal Layton

| Little Archie and the Spectacular Disaster-Magnet TV Gadget | 978-0-330-44779-9 | £3.99 |
| Little Archie and the Tongue-Tingling Super-Shrinking Powder | 978-0-330-44189-6 | £3.99 |
